THE

SHAPE

OF

SECRETS

Willow River Press is an imprint of Between the Lines Publishing. The Willow River Press name and logo are trademarks of Between the Lines Publishing.

Between the Lines Publishing
1769 Lexington Ave N, Ste 286
Roseville MN 55113
btwnthelines.com

First Published: January 2024

ISBN: Paperback 978-1-958901-74-8

ISBN: Ebook 978-1-958901-75-5

Library of Congress Control Number: 2023948062

THE

SHAPE

OF

SECRETS

Eileen Riley Hall

This book is dedicated to my heroes, my amazing daughters, Elizabeth Anne, and Caroline Grace. Love you always.

Gone...

They found the body hidden in the trees, hastily buried under leaves, in the mud. A person I loved so much was suddenly gone. That summer, I couldn't hide anymore. That summer, I had to learn to be brave. And so, I did...

I Can't Explain

Friday, June 23, 1972

My mother never believed me. About anything.

Truth was what she willed it to be, and the day of my sixth-grade graduation was no exception.

"Where are your friends, Margaret Grace?" my mother demanded, her voice threaded with irritation at even having to ask the question.

"I don't have any school friends," I mumbled, pained at having to say aloud what was obvious to everyone else.

"That's ridiculous. You must have some girlfriends. You have been going to school here for seven years!" my mother exclaimed, her arms gesturing in frustration at the brick school building behind us. She eyed me suspiciously, as if I were willfully hiding a secret coven of giggling girlfriends from her.

My mother's blistering stare added to the heat of the blazing sun as I stood sweltering on the front lawn of my school, Saint Christopher's Catholic Academy in Milford, New York. The half-Mass, half-assembly graduation was over, and the nuns had ushered us from the stifling cafeteria to the oppressive heat outside for a reception. June had decided to be exceptionally steamy that year, making an already unpleasant day that much worse.

In typical nun fashion, the reception was a stingy, spartan event where guests were offered rapidly melting ice cream sandwiches and warm, watery lemonade. Scattered around us on the lawn were the Dominican sisters who ran the school, and my classmates, many of whom were holding awards they received for math, science, athleticism, and citizenship. It had not escaped my mother's attention that I received no such award.

"Look around," my mother instructed with a commanding wave of her hand. "There is obviously someone you're not thinking about."

I could look from here to California, and my answer would be the same, so I just shrugged in reply. Besides, I was too exhausted, dejected, and sweaty to find words to explain my perpetually friendless state.

I looked to my 16-year-old sister Patty and my grandmother, desperate for support or at least a distraction, but they were as overheated and unhappy as I was.

Grandma appeared to be wilting as she wiped beads of perspiration — and most of her face powder — from her brow with a lace handkerchief. The event had put her in an irritable mood. She alternated between looking at the sky, predicting rain and checking her watch as if she was late for a very important appointment. At least Grandma's disapproval was largely silent, punctuated only by deep sighs and a sour expression.

My sister Patty stood sulking next to our grandmother. She and our mother had already sparred about the skimpy pink sundress Patty was wearing. Patty snuck the sundress by our mother by putting a cardigan over it as we left the house. On all occasions, but especially when it involved school or church, our mother enforced a strict dress code that required convent modesty. The June heat forced Patty to remove the cardigan halfway through the ceremony, and as she did, our mother gasped as if Patty had performed a striptease in full view of the nuns.

In return, Patty rolled her eyes and assumed her standard pose: arms folded, face registering both boredom and irritation. She began picking at the purple polish on her fingernails, a habit which drove our mother crazy. My sister had perfected the art of being an insolent teenager.

My father, the only marginally pleasant member of my family, had opted out of this occasion, preferring to work, and now I think we all understood why.

Remarkably, my mother—dressed in her standard, conservative, navy-blue dress—wasn't sweating at all. She likely considered perspiration a moral failure. Instead, she stood cool and aloof, hands on hips, awaiting a satisfactory response from me.

"Well," she said, expectantly.

"I don't have any friends here," I hissed through gritted teeth, slowly enunciating each word to her. Her eyes startled at my tone. I was not usually so bold.

"Don't take this out on me, young lady. You don't even try," she sniped, turning her laser focus to the crowd on the lawn, and squinting her eyes in steely determination.

I suppose as we were standing in sight of the Virgin Mary statue, my mother felt she deserved a friend miracle, or at least a classmate to pose for a picture with me. That way she could put a respectable photo on the mantel and pretend I was the daughter she wanted.

But it had already been a long, hot, hopeless afternoon, and it showed no signs of improving anytime soon.

I started the day with foolish optimism as graduation was one occasion when I wasn't required to wear my very unflattering school uniform, its plaid kilt, knee socks, and white blouse with capped sleeves mocking my shape. So, the week before I had chosen a purple, gypsy-inspired dress from the mall. I hoped the dress could transform me into a hippie goddess.

But the dress was a disaster in real life. It was too tight on my middle, constricting my round stomach, and kept flying up in the breeze to reveal my chubby thighs. As much as I wanted to resemble my tall, skinny peers who looked effortlessly cool in everything they wore, I was short and still had what my mother referred to as "baby fat," a term that made it no less unattractive. I was still awaiting the mythical growth spurt that would

3

anoint me with long limbs and curves in the right places. But not only had it not happened; it wasn't even a glint on the horizon.

Even worse was my hair. My classmates all seemed to have long, straight silky manes, like Barbie dolls or wild ponies. But my hair was dark, curly, and—despite my efforts at styling—formed a ratty ball at the back of my head when I attempted to tame it into a pretty ponytail.

At least I had hair now. My mother, having silky hair, didn't know what to do with my wild hair when I was a little girl, so she kept it super short. She told me it was short like Mia Farrow's, a beautiful actress married to Frank Sinatra. Mia had lovely shiny blonde hair and looked like Tinkerbell.

But my hair was just a curly mess atop my head, making me look like a mangy little boy. By third grade, I refused any more scalpings. Of course, my hair didn't just grow longer; it grew bigger. But at least people knew I was a girl.

I traced my mother's gaze as it landed on the most popular and prettiest girl in my class.

"Oh look, there's Jessica," my mother's voice brightened as she began to wave to the queen of the 6th grade. Jessica had come to my house to play a couple of times when we were in kindergarten, and my mother assumed this created a lifelong connection. She was wrong. Jessica had catapulted out of my orbit long ago.

"Mom, no, please," I tried to head off this impending humiliation. But it was no use.

"Jessica," my mother called out enthusiastically, and I cringed.

I pushed stray hairs off my face and attempted to reinsert them into my ponytail. I could almost feel my hair growing larger as Jessica approached us.

Beautiful blonde Jessica floated over with a big smile. Her long pink dress cinched her tiny waist and billowed behind her like a train. Jessica had never treated me cruelly; she was above that. That was the job of the middle management girls—the social climbers. She simply ignored me.

4

"Hello, Mrs. Murphy. Hi, Maggie. Congratulations!" Jessica greeted me with the false friendliness all my peers feigned in the presence of adults. My mother and Jessica began a pleasant conversation about school and her favorite classes. I wondered how this girl who saw my mother a few times a year could have a better rapport with her than I did.

"Congratulations on all your awards, Jessica! Very impressive," my mother gushed.

"Oh, it was nothing. Lots of kids got awards, maybe not as many, but still," Jessica answered demurely, and I suddenly felt even worse. Until that moment, I hadn't thought I could feel worse.

"What are you doing to celebrate, Jessica?" my mother inquired, and my grandmother studied the scene as if she were a director in a small play, anxiously awaiting the next line.

"Well, we are having a pool party at my house," Jessica offered tentatively. "My parents ordered subs and most of the class is coming over."

Of course, they were. The entire class would be thrilled to spend the day at Jessica's perfect house, in Jessica's perfect, sparkling pool. It was like an invitation to Buckingham Palace.

I knew about this party; the entire class had been invited, as the nuns insisted on the courtesy that an invitation to any class event be extended to every child. But just as firm as that policy was the kid rule that dictated you did not go where you were not wanted.

No one expected me at that party, nor wanted me to go. I certainly never mentioned it to my mother. The thought of trying to pretend I fit in with my peers for hours at a pool party was torturous to me. Although Jessica would be cordial to me in the distant kind of way a queen is with her subjects, I had no doubt the girls who liked to mock me would be in attendance.

Everyone stared at me, expecting a response.

"Oh, yeah, well, I'm meeting Richie after this, at his house," I quickly countered, looking down and grinding my sandal into an anthill in the grass.

I could feel my mother grimace, as if a cartoon cloud formed above her head.

"Nonsense, Maggie," my mother dismissed my plans. Then she turned to Jessica to answer for me.

"She'd love to come. Thank you, Jessica," my mother responded, offering her a wide smile and ignoring the fact that Jessica hadn't specifically asked me to come.

I felt my cheeks burning with shame and wished I could disappear.

"Well, see you there, Maggie," Jessica smiled and walked away to join her hive of worshipful friends. I was mortified.

"Oh my God, Mom, you totally humiliated the kid!" Patty interjected loudly. "No 12-year-old wants her mother getting her invited to parties!"

Although my older sister was often my persecutor, she could at times be on my side when it came to our overbearing mother and delighted in aggravating her in the process. My way of dealing with my mother was to stay clear of her critical eye as much as possible. My sister took her on directly. I admired my sister's spunk.

My grandmother felt the need to smooth it over, "Well, I think the girl seemed very happy to have Maggie at her party," she offered cluelessly. Then she smiled at me and gave me a quick pat on the back.

Ignoring reality was pretty much Grandma's greatest talent; she also had a gift for making me feel like the pathetic runt in a litter of kittens. Her comment reignited my perpetual resentment of her. Grandma was short and round, and I blamed her chunky genes for my unfortunate figure. Both of my parents were tall and slim.

"Mom, I told Richie I'd meet him right after this at his house. Grandma Rose is making a cake for me!" I protested, and it came out shriller than I intended.

I saw her flinch, and knew I'd said the wrong thing. I didn't understand why my mother was always so negative about Richie when he was my best friend in the entire universe, and a thousand times better than all the Jessicas in the world.

"Well, *your* grandma is right here," she shot back, effectively shaming me for my affection for Richie's grandma. She then continued her rebuttal, "and we have a cake from the bakery. You can have it after the party. Besides, it isn't healthy for a nearly teenage girl to spend all her time with a ......boy." She said "boy" as if she wasn't exactly sure that's what Richie was.

"I don't even have my bathing suit!" I argued in frustration, not that I would have worn a bathing suit in front of my classmates for all the money in the world. Chubby and flat-chested was not a winning look. If I had to put on a bathing suit, why not just show up in one of Grandma's skirted bathing suits with the pointy cone boobs and declare my life officially over?

"We can stop home for your suit. You're going," she announced and marched off towards the car to signal that the conversation was over. My grandmother and my sister followed, and I trudged behind, miserable. I opened the car door slowly and slumped in the backseat. I could see my mother's scowl in the rearview mirror and felt the weight of her disappointment as she silently drove away from school.

My mother would never understand my hopeless school life. I just didn't fit in there. It started in kindergarten because I had a tendency to cry over small things. Teasing me to bring on the tears became a favorite pastime of my peers.

But it was one October day in first grade that sealed my fate as an outsider. For once, I had actually been invited to play freeze tag with a few girls from my class. Thrilled at having been included, I didn't want to leave the game to use the bathroom. Unfortunately, I overestimated the strength of my bladder. I tried to hide my humiliating accident, but when we lined up to go back inside, all the girls laughed at the wet streaks on my bare legs. Stupid Catholic school uniforms skirts.

"Maggie needs a diaper," one girl cackled at me.

After my public humiliation on the playground, I made lots of trips to the girls' room at school, just to make sure I never had another accident. Accidents were not unfamiliar to me. I was a bedwetter through second grade, a failing I had been scolded for by my mother many times. But even my attempts to avoid another accident became a source of torment. The refrain, "Maggie's in the bathroom" became a joke among my peers when a nun would ask where I was.

After that, I pretty much stayed in my own orbit, playing alone on the swings, or keeping my head in a book—better there than on the chopping block again. I was lonely, but I chose distance rather than hazard an attempt at friendship. Fear of rejection kept me alone. Shame clung to me like dark magic. Maybe the other kids could sense it and that was the real reason that they rejected me. We had spent seven years together, but the best I could hope for was a kind of icy politeness. They would never be my friends.

As we sped along in my mother's car, I wondered how long I would have to stay at the party before my mother would agree to come and get me. And I wished more than anything I was riding my bike to see Richie.

Wonder Twins

Richie Harper and I met at the Little League field when I was seven and he was six. Patty and I went to a game because she had a crush on a boy in her class named Frank Mulroney. That was back when an 11-year-old Patty didn't mind taking me to places like the playground or for ice cream at dinky Watson's Market on the corner.

It was a Friday night in May, and I was sitting in the stands watching the Pee-Wee League before the main event. This little kid in a #5 uniform ran faster than anyone I had ever seen. Even though it was only the Pee-Wee League, the entire crowd was cheering, mesmerized by this boy who sped like a rocket around the bases. They were shouting, "Number Five's Alive!" I marveled at what it would be like to be so good at something that people created a cheer just for you.

But soon enough, the Pee-Wee game was over, and with it any excitement. My sister became engrossed in swooning over Frank, who as far as I could tell was just a chubby boy with a mullet haircut who couldn't hit the ball. I was bored, so I left the stands and walked over to the playground that adjoined the field.

To my surprise, I found #5 hanging from the monkey bars. He waved at me upside down. I was wary because he was a boy and an athlete, and I was a shy, uncoordinated girl with no brothers.

After effortlessly flipping himself upright, he smiled at me. I immediately noticed that his two front teeth protruded a bit more than the rest, and he had dimples so big they looked almost cartoonish. The combined effect was quirky and charming.

"I'm Richie," he offered with a little wave.

"Maggie," I replied hesitantly. He seemed to ponder me for a moment and then, apparently finding me acceptable, he just began to talk.

"Can you dance? Cause I can. I'm going to be a dancer one day," Richie shared with a broad smile.

"Um, not well," I answered, looking down and kicking the sand under the monkey bars.

"Well, I can teach you," he answered brightly.

And right there on the playground in view of the whole world, he started to dance. And he was good, like *American Bandstand* good. He tried to teach me a few steps from a Temptations song, and I awkwardly attempted to imitate him. But he seemed oblivious to my lack of talent, just happy to have someone to dance with him.

We spent the rest of that evening on the swings, comparing favorite songs, TV shows (we both loved *Bewitched*), and talking about our schools and families. Richie had attended first grade at Milford Public Elementary School that year. He had an older brother, Charlie, and an older sister, Monica, and his grandmother lived with the family. His dad was a mechanic and his mom a nurse. As he rambled on, I just kept smiling and thanking God that this unusual person had selected me for a friend.

Despite his athletic talent, Richie's little league days were numbered. He quit after that one season. He didn't enjoy playing, and the other boys on the team didn't seem to like Richie, excluding him from their celebrations and friendships.

The baseball team's loss was my greatest gain. I had found my best friend.

Knowing Richie changed my life. Someone finally knew me and–even better–liked me. When everything else in my life was a dingy black and white, Richie was in Technicolor.

Once we figured out the way to each other's houses, we quickly became inseparable. We played Barbies and baby dolls. Baked half-raw desserts in my Easy Bake Oven, watching the tiny chocolate cakes rise under the heat from the dim lightbulb. Listened to records in my garage and his, and practiced dances to all our favorite songs on the radio. Richie was my dance teacher, and I was his only student, clumsy and hapless as I might be.

I was so uncoordinated that when Richie instructed me to raise my arm during one of our dances, I often kicked my foot first.

Richie was wiry and agile, always moving to an internal rhythm and effortlessly copying complicated dance moves we saw on TV. After watching a dance just one time on *American Bandstand*, he could replicate the entire thing. His bony little legs would kick, and his body would twist and turn with the music as if he was part of the song. And the entire time he danced, he would be smiling, his brown eyes twinkling.

Despite all our outward differences, I felt more comfortable with Richie than anyone else in my life. From the moment we met, we just understood each other. As we grew older, I confided in him my secret dream of becoming a writer, and he had no doubt I could do it. He thought I was great, and I thought he was the most interesting, talented, and kindest person on the planet.

But from the first time I brought Richie over to my house, my mother wasn't happy.

Richie wasn't Catholic; he was Baptist. He attended public school, which according to my mother was full of hooligans and heathens. His parents were not friends of hers; he didn't live in our neighborhood; and he was Black. In my mother's critical eyes, I am sure his race alone made him an unsuitable best friend, although she would never admit to it or say it outright.

Now that we were 11 and 12 respectively, our friendship was getting more criticism from my mother. Richie was getting taller, though no heftier, and I was in my mother's words, "on the cusp of becoming a young lady." The phrase evoked images of white gloves, tea parties, and learning to iron, all of which sounded god-awful and boring to me.

My mother had insinuated on more than one occasion that a plump, awkward girl, and skinny, hyperactive boy looked unseemly palling around together. She couldn't see that Richie and I understood each other in a way no one else did. We were, in the truest sense of the words, best friends.

One of our favorite cartoons was the *Wonder Twins*, a spinoff from the *Superfriends* with Superman and Batman. The Wonder Twins were magic together; when they fist-bumped, they could become anything in the universe. That's how Richie and I felt, and we often re-enacted the fist-bump and imagined all the cool things we could do and be together.

We had already decided this was going to be our best summer ever because so many exciting things were happening—the Summer Olympics, a solar eclipse, and a sense of newfound freedom as we hovered on the brink of becoming teenagers. The world seemed wide open, full of thrilling possibilities.

Don't Pee in the Pool

As we pulled into our driveway, I made another attempt to plead my case about the pool party, but my mother would hear no arguments. She ordered me into the house to change into my bathing suit, stubbornly leaving the car running. I dug the only bathing suit that fit me out of my closet. It was a bright yellow one-piece that made me look like a bloated lemon. I put my dress back on over it and had zero intention of ever taking it off.

When I got back to the car, I saw that my grandmother and sister hopped off the misery train at our house, so I was forced to sit in the front seat with my mother. We rode in silence through the city streets where I lived and into the suburbs inhabited by my wealthier classmates. As we pulled into the driveway at Jessica's huge colonial house— with the pristine white fence surrounding a generous backyard—my mother offered her intimidating version of a pep talk, with a semi-threatening smile.

"Put yourself out there. Talk to people. Find some girlfriends! I'll be back in two hours." She commanded a short list of miracles as she prodded me out of the car, then drove away at what seemed an alarmingly fast rate. I watched her car disappear around the corner and felt defeated.

I slunk through the gate into Jessica's back yard. I surveyed the scene for a few minutes from a safe distance. All the girls from my class were lying on towels in the grass in their tiny bikinis as the boys splashed and swam in the pool. Occasionally the two groups yelled at each other, or a boy traipsed over to the island of towels and shook his wet hair on the squealing girls. It was a mating ritual that left me clueless and alone.

Eventually, the girls spotted me, so I was obligated to go over and attempt to make conversation. Jessica was in the middle of the group, telling a story when I approached. I sat near the edge of their towels, gave a hesitant wave, and listened to their conversation as I absentmindedly picked blades of grass from her perfect lawn and wished for time to pass at the speed of light.

"I'm pretty sure he likes me. He's been calling like, every night," Jessica shared with a satisfied smile and a toss of her beautiful hair. Her bikini was hot pink, and she somehow managed to be extremely thin yet still have boobs. Life was so unfair.

"Of course, he likes you! Duh! Why wouldn't he? You're like, perfect," spouted Jackie, one of Jessica's best friends and ladies-in-waiting. Jackie was a smaller, less pretty version of Jessica, with a slight overbite and a nose that needed to stop growing sooner rather than later.

Soon all the girls were reassuring Jessica that any boy would be lucky to have her as a girlfriend, and she was feigning embarrassment at all the praise. I just sat silently, hoping the two hours would pass with me as an unobtrusive observer. But I would not be so lucky.

One of the meaner girls, Lydia, spotted me. Lydia had long dark hair practically to her butt and always wore very expensive clothes. But she wasn't pretty. She had small eyes, a fat nose, and her pink face was always fighting a losing battle with acne. It seemed to put her in a permanently nasty mood. Her eyes squinted as she took in my appearance with disdain. The straps of my yellow bathing suit clashed badly with my purple dress, and the yellow color beneath the purple combined to make parts of the dress look murky brown. Could I be any more of an oddity?

"What about you, Maggie? Who do you like?" she asked me, and in unison all the other girls stopped talking and looked at me to hear my response. I could feel my cheeks burning up. I had no idea what to say. I thought for a minute about what would be the safest answer and decided to go with a pop star.

"Oh, I just like Donny Osmond," I offered casually. My response elicited uproarious laughter.

"C'mon, Maggie. We're not little kids anymore," Lydia sneered. "There must be someone you like? At least I *hope* there's a boy you like," she said slyly. And I could see the trap she had set.

If I didn't give her a name, she would begin to trot out the theory that I didn't like boys at all, and that would only lead to permanent ostracization and torment. But if I gave her a name, she would delight in telling the boy so he could reject me publicly. I felt myself start to sweat.

"Well, there is one guy, but he's older," I offered vaguely. That sparked Jackie's interest.

"Who? Tell us, Maggie. We'll keep your secret. Girl code," she said with false sincerity and crossed her wicked heart. The only girl code I knew was that girls had generally agreed to be mean to me. But I was stuck. I was a chubby baby seal among circling sharks. Damn my mother for making me come to this witches' coven.

"His name is Charlie," I said, and they all looked confused, trying to identify a Charlie in our school.

"Charlie Fitzsimmons?" Lydia asked, horrified and delighted because Charlie Fitzsimmons was a freshman and a football star. Horrified because he was light-years above my social status, delighted because he would no doubt resoundingly reject me.

"No, Charlie Harper," I answered, hoping that would be the end of it.

Charlie Harper was Richie's older brother and my future husband, if I had any say in it. He was as handsome as a pop star in *Tiger Beat* magazine, with what Richie's Grandma Rose called a hundred-watt smile. He was tall, with a big afro, and twinkling brown eyes. Charlie was athletic and had been a star on both the soccer and baseball teams in high school, but he also had an amazing voice. As he worked on his car in the Harpers' driveway, I could hear him singing old Sam Cook songs, and I would just about faint on the sidewalk. I was in love with him, and I fantasized that when we were older, and I was finally skinny with better hair, we would get married.

I assumed not many of my Catholic school classmates knew Richie's family well enough to know his older brother's name. The Harpers were lowly, public-school attendees after all. I thought I was safe. Then Jackie's eyes grew wide with delight.

"Oh my God, you mean the colored Charlie! Your weirdo friend Richie's brother," she shrieked, and they all began to laugh at me. Suddenly, they all knew exactly who I was referring to.

"Don't say colored. Say Black," I sputtered to correct her.

Charlie had explained to me once why Black was the right word, when I said my grandma said colored. It had to do with Black people choosing what they wanted to be called. I understood completely because I had spent many years wishing my name was anything cooler than Margaret Grace, which was certainly a nun name if I ever heard one. Just another favor my mother had done me.

"Isn't that guy like 25? What a creep!" Jackie screeched.

"He's 19, and I didn't say I was dating him, just that I liked him," I tried to explain.

"Um, yeah, no need to explain. We knew *you* weren't dating anyone, Maggie," Lydia cackled in disgust. Bored of mocking me, the other girls started up the conversation about Jessica's love life again. I got up to walk away, and someone shouted, "Don't pee in the pool." I would never live down my first-grade humiliation.

I kept my head down and made a beeline for the snack table on the stone patio. I found a chair under the awning and sat down in earshot of the adults to provide a buffer from the girls. They couldn't taunt me with all their parents right there. A couple of times, adults reminded me that the kids were either in the pool or on the lawn. It was evident that they wanted their cocktail party to themselves.

"You know, sweetie, the kids are all over there," a woman in a floppy pink hat who appeared slightly inebriated directed me toward the pool.

"I can't be in the sun. I have a rare skin condition," I lied to her, my voice solemn, but she looked at me with irritation.

"Well, then, you probably shouldn't be at a pool party," she said with a sneer. I bet if she had a daughter, she was a mean girl. Her hat flopped over her eyes, and her crooked nose protruded like a Halloween witch.

But I didn't budge because at least the adults couldn't be overtly mean. I smiled at all the adults who came by, and I proceeded to eat an entire bowl of M&M's. Eventually, I figured it had to be close to the time my mother would be arriving. And I was weary of watching my socially superior classmates laugh and flirt. It was too painful.

So, I walked around to the front of the house and stood on the porch. Jessica's sweet gray cat found me, and I sat on a rocker petting her cat until my mother finally showed up.

As my mother's blue Ford pulled in the driveway, I could see the disappointment on her face from the steps. I was a social failure, and we both knew it. I trudged to the car and got in silently. We exchanged a look of mutual misery, but no words were spoken. My mother was an erratic driver at best, but in a sour mood, she was downright dangerous. The ride home was more rollercoaster than car ride, and I held onto the car door as she careened through the streets, jerking to an abrupt stop in our driveway.

Best Babysitter Ever

My luck changed when I got out of the car because I saw Gina coming out of a neighbor's house. Evangelina "Gina" Russo had been my babysitter for years before my sister was old enough to watch me.

Even though my mother didn't work, she was often out volunteering at school and church, and she kept a busy social calendar with dinner parties and bridge nights. I was grateful my mother liked to leave the house because Gina was one of my favorite people on the planet, and I wanted to grow up to be just like her. She was beautiful with long light brown hair and blue eyes, but more than that she was sweet and fun, and she genuinely liked me.

Most babysitters just put on the TV and called a friend or boy to talk on the phone all night. But when Gina babysat, we played all kinds of games, including a version of the gameshow *The Price is Right* she made up just for me because it was one of my favorite shows.

I would pretend to "Come on Down" and she would have me guess at the price of household items in our kitchen. If I won, she would have candy prizes for me. Patty loved Gina too, and even now when Patty saw Gina, Patty's old smile would return, and I could glimpse my sweet sister hidden behind the rebellious teenage exterior.

Lots of nights when she was babysitting, Gina would let Richie come over. I'm not sure my mother appreciated Gina's independent decision to allow Richie to join in the evening, but my mother knew Gina was babysitter gold, and she didn't want to rock the boat, especially when her bridge night was at stake.

When Richie played *The Price is Right* with us, he would get as hyper as the contestants on the real show. We would all laugh so hard at his antics as he jumped around, guessing at the price of flour or pretzels. Gina would always walk Richie home afterward, and he would share some of his best dance moves on the way. He loved her as much as we did. Gina knew Richie's whole family. She was in the same graduating class as Charlie at Milford High School, and they had been close friends since they were in grade school.

Gina was 19 now and wanted to be an elementary school teacher, and I knew she would be an amazing teacher. She was coming out of our neighbors' house, the Johnsons, when I spied her. She was their babysitter now.

Mr. Johnson was an English teacher at Milford High School, and his wife and he had a beautiful baby with blonde hair and chubby cheeks. The baby's name was Daisy, after some character in a book that Mr. Johnson loved. Both Mr. and Mrs. Johnson looked like TV stars. She was small and waiflike, with long blonde hair, pale skin, and perfect white teeth. She was so tiny; from a distance, she looked like a child.

Mr. Johnson was very tall and handsome with deep brown eyes and feathered dark hair that came to his shoulders. When the Johnsons moved in two summers ago, my mother brought over a pie to welcome them, and my sister and I tagged along out of curiosity. We were mesmerized by how perfect they both were. Rumor had it that all the girls in the 11th grade were in love with Mr. Johnson, and I could see why.

But Mr. Johnson only had eyes for his wife. In the evenings, Mrs. Johnson would usually wait on the front porch for her husband, baby on her hip. When Mr. Johnson arrived home from work, he would bounce up the front steps of their house, often with flowers in his hand, and dip his wife in a kiss like a movie star. He always referred to her as "my beautiful bride." And the way he looked at her made me blush.

The ladies of the neighborhood were often outside when Mr. Johnson arrived home, and there was a collective sigh as this romantic scene unfolded. Even my mother seemed to swoon a bit in his presence. More than one evening at dinner, she would casually mention that Mr. Johnson gave his wife, "the most beautiful bouquet of lilies this evening," and my dad would ignore the comment as best he could.

When I got out of the car, Gina was standing on the sidewalk in front of the Johnsons' house, talking to Mr. Johnson. He must have been saying something funny because she threw her head back in a laugh. They continued to chat for a minute, and I politely waited for them to finish their conversation. My mother stood next to me watching them, her eyes narrowed critically. She made it her business to evaluate all human interactions on our street. Finally, Mr. Johnson gave Gina a little wave and hopped back up his front steps. She turned toward the street.

"Gina!" I hollered happily to her.

"Hey, Maggie May," Gina called to me, waving both arms above her head. She had been calling me Maggie May since the Rod Stewart song hit the airwaves the summer before. I loved it because I finally had a counterpart name to her nickname for Richie, Little Richard.

I ran from my mom over to Gina on the other side of the street. I hugged her, and she kissed the top of my head. Gina and my mom exchanged polite waves from across the street.

In the old days, my mother would have come over to chat with Gina too, but something had changed in the past couple of years. My mother had remarked a few times that Gina was "losing her way," and referenced her wild boyfriend and the Vietnam War protests Gina attended. But I knew better. Gina was still the same sweet person she had always been.

Gina looked as pretty as ever in old jeans and a Rolling Stones t-shirt. She was already tan, and her hair—streaked blonde from the sun—was tucked in a loose bun at the back of her neck. Long limbed and graceful,

Gina's only flaw was slightly crooked teeth, but that just seemed to make her prettier because she wasn't perfect. She was Gina. She was my role model, idol, and another sister to me.

"I miss you!" I told her.

"What have you and Little Richard been up to?" she asked with a smile.

"Well, we almost have the entire dance to 'I Got You Back' memorized, but Richie is better than I am at it by a mile. And we are learning to roller-skate, although I mostly just fall down a lot. If we get good enough, we're going to the rink in town this summer," I offered happily.

"Sounds like a blast," she said and then examined my dress.

"I had to get dressed up," I explained in embarrassment.

"I love your dress. It's so bohemian and cool. You look beautiful! I might be mistaken, but I think you graduated from sixth grade today," she joked and produced a card from her purse.

"Aw, Gina, you didn't have to do that," I said, but my smile belied how happy I was that she remembered.

"I was going to leave this in your mailbox, but I'm in luck running into you!" she beamed.

I took the card. Gina had written my name on the envelope in beautiful calligraphy with hearts and balloons drawn around it. The card featured Snoopy and Woodstock in graduation gowns and tucked inside was a five-dollar bill. We both loved the Peanuts comics. When Gina used to babysit, she would often show up with a Peanuts comic she cut out of the newspaper for me. She knew I liked the Sally comics the best.

"Thanks, Gina!" I said, so grateful for her thoughtfulness.

"Well, I know you are super into music now, so I thought you could buy some records. Maybe the new one by Donny Osmond," she suggested, smiling.

"Definitely, and some other records too with this," I replied, and shook the fresh five-dollar bill happily. Five dollars could buy at least five singles. I was already compiling a list of songs in my head.

Just then, Gina's boyfriend Ray pulled up, his car radio blasting Alice Cooper's "School's Out." My mother said Ray was "no good." He was handsome, for sure, with long sandy brown hair, nearly as long as Gina's, and bright blue eyes like Bobby Sherman, another pop idol I loved. Grandma said Ray looked like Jimmy Dean, but I found no resemblance to the sausage king. Then Patty explained to me that Grandma meant James Dean, a movie actor who died in the 50's. Patty said Grandma lived on another planet and never got anything right.

Unlike Gina, Ray had no plans to go to college. He painted houses with his father, so his arms were muscular and tan, and his hair was perpetually specked with white and blue paint. Despite Ray's good looks, he was kind of rough and not very friendly. He drove a shiny red Trans Am, and the engine was thunderous when he gunned it. My mother said Gina chose bad guys because her dad left when she was little, and she had low self-worth. I wasn't sure about any of that, but I did think she could find a guy nicer than Ray.

Ray's car idled as we stood on the sidewalk. I sort of waved at him, and he waved back begrudgingly.

"Well, I gotta go," Gina motioned to the car. "Ray and I are going to a party tonight. But we will catch up soon," Gina promised and hugged me again quickly.

Ray didn't even get out to open her door, just honked on the horn for her to hurry up. No sooner had Gina shut the door than Ray rocketed the car out of our neighborhood. I knew my mother would be rolling her eyes at the roar of his engine.

I watched them drive away and walked off in the direction of Richie's house. I usually took my bike because his house was a good distance away, but I didn't want to risk going back for it and have my mom ask where I was going. As it turned out, I didn't have to go far before I found Richie one block over, on a dead-end street that was adjacent to one of the walking paths to the public school. Richie and I often met there to sit on the fence and discuss life.

Richie was cross-legged in the middle of the road, popping tar bubbles. Popping tar bubbles was a common pastime of ours when we couldn't find anything else to do. The city would fill potholes with tar, and in the summer, the potholes would remain a bubbling liquid for a while before semi-solidifying. They made an especially satisfying mini explosion when you squashed them. This particular dead-end street was a good spot because cars rarely drove down it.

I plopped down next to Richie and imagined my mother's face in a tar bubble before I exploded it with my thumb. He looked up at me and smiled.

"Hey," I said. "I'm sorry I didn't come by. My mother forced me to go to a stupid party after graduation," I apologized. He shrugged.

"I wondered what happened. It's okay," he reassured me, and I knew he wasn't mad.

"Who had the party?" Richie asked, looking up at me. I sighed.

"Mean girls from school. It was awful," I explained, shaking my head.

"Sorry, Mags," he consoled me. I knew Richie had his own troubles at school although he was uncharacteristically vague on the topic. He would share his love of English and science class with me, but he never mentioned friends. Gina told me kids teased and excluded him at school, a fate I knew all too well.

"I hope Grandma Rose isn't upset I didn't get to your house for the cake," I mumbled, worried I had disappointed her. But I knew that was unlikely with Grandma Rose. She was all warmth and hugs.

"Nah, she said you could come over any day for it. She's keeping it in the fridge to make sure it's fresh. She even made little cakes for Sonny and Cher," he rolled his eyes at the mention of our old baby dolls.

Sonny and Cher were "twin" Baby Tender Love dolls I named after the married pop duo because I loved Cher, the beautiful singer. Sonny and Cher had a variety show on Sunday nights that I watched with my parents. My mother hated it because Cher always began the show in a gown and then stripped it off to reveal some glittering, scanty dress. My mother always frowned and sighed in disapproval, but my dad would smile.

I received a blonde Baby Tender Love doll for my birthday in second grade, and that Christmas, I asked Santa for a Black Baby Tender Love Doll. I wanted my blonde girl to have a brother. My mother said Santa gave children dolls that looked like them, but I said I knew Santa would not let me down.

In the end, I supposed she relented because she didn't want to seem petty or prejudiced, and there was probably some nudging by my dad. So, on Christmas morning that year, I opened a red present with a green ribbon to find my beautiful Black Baby Tender Love doll. I was thrilled.

Later that afternoon, after Christmas Mass and an early dinner, I ran over to Richie's house with my new doll. His parents exchanged puzzled smiles when I showed my doll to them, but his Grandma Rose took my doll in her arms and rocked him. "You have a beautiful baby, Maggie," she said to me, and I beamed.

Richie and I spent many days playing house with Sonny and Cher in my garage. There was an old blue couch and a dirty yellow kitchen table and chairs in our garage that belonged to my father's parents.

We would rock and feed our babies, "cook" dinner, and generally create our own domestic paradise of two, plus the doll babies. It never seemed strange to me that Richie liked to play baby dolls and Barbies, or color, or roller-skate with me. The other kids would tease us, calling me a freak and Richie a sissy, but so long as I had Richie, I could ignore them. Sonny and Cher still had a place of honor on my bed, and I was pleased Grandma Rose had remembered to bake cakes for them.

"So, what are we going to do this summer?" I asked him, as I pictured Lydia's pink face in the next tar bubble I popped.

Last summer we spent a good amount of time riding our bikes over the giant mounds of dirt left by construction crews that were building new houses on the side of town closest to the suburbs. On those days, my mother would send me straight to the shower before she would let me near anything else in the house. But this summer I already felt restless for more exciting activities.

24

"Let's walk to my house. Grandma Rose said she had chocolate ice cream for us too," Richie suggested. He was a chocolate ice cream fiend, and Grandma Rose was generous with her scoops.

We walked in an easy silence to his house, and he scurried inside, returning with two sugar cones bursting with ice cream. As we ate our cones, Richie jumped up to show me a new dance he had seen, ice cream dripping down his face.

"Watch this! It's awesome!" He started dancing in the street, and I laughed. Pretty soon, he pulled me up and showed me the steps. It was our mission to watch *American Bandstand* and *Soul Train* every Saturday to come up with new dances. If we got good enough at a dance, Richie said we could enter the Talent Show at Milford Junior High in the fall. I couldn't imagine ever getting on a stage in front of people, but with Richie at my side, maybe I could try.

We stayed in the road practicing the steps until I figured it was dinner time. We parted with a wave, and I felt happy as I walked home. No matter what the summer held, Richie and I would be in it together.

Dinner and a Show

As soon as I got to the sidewalk in front of our old four-square house, I could hear my parents fighting. This was pretty much a nightly ritual, but it usually didn't start until after dinner.

Patty was waiting for me at the front door. Her arms were crossed, and she rolled her eyes at me.

"Hey, the drama started early tonight. Something about Mom wanting a new car," she said with an exaggerated sigh. I wondered if my mother's aggressive driving had damaged her car.

"Where's Grandma?" I asked, not really caring either way.

"She bolted when they started picking at each other, claiming a headache," Patty snickered and shook her head. Grandma was an expert at sensing emotional pressure drops. A lifetime of difficult people had honed her senses well. We would likely all have headaches before the night was done.

"She left you that plant thing as a gift," Patty laughed at the absurd present, pointing at a small violet plant on the coffee table. And I followed Patty into the living room.

"Oh, that was nice," I remarked blandly.

"Yeah, just what every 12-year-old wants. A stupid plant. Oh, and a card with 5 bucks in it. Really breaking the old bank," Patty said sarcastically.

26

I was slightly annoyed that Patty had opened my card. I knew she would never take the money; it was the principle of the thing. But my sister was nothing if not nosy.

"What's for dinner?" I asked, wondering if this early fight time meant we wouldn't be having dinner. It had happened before. After one pre-dinner fight, my mother abandoned a raw chicken on the kitchen counter. It sat for about an hour before my dad put it in the trash, slamming the back screen door as he threw it out.

"Dad just went out back to grill burgers. There's a brief intermission between acts," my sister shared with a mocking laugh.

I stood in our living room, unsure what to do next. My mother tried to keep our living room formal with a stiff floral couch, two wingback chairs, a glass top coffee table, and a China cabinet full of plates and crystal glasses we only used on Christmas and Easter.

The TV was also in the living room. My mother resented the clunky TV invading the sanctity of her room and would snap it off mid program if the mood suited her. Usually, Patty and I flopped on the floor to watch TV. It was easier than sitting on the sofa and having our mother watch to make sure neither our feet, nor any crumbs or spills, blemished her one expensive piece of furniture.

The sofa was a Stickley, as my mother frequently reminded us, her eyebrows arched for emphasis. I had no idea what a Stickley was, but at times I thought she loved that sofa more than my sister or me. Our house was old, but my mother did her best to make it look as nice as possible, and her standards for cleanliness were of a royal caliber. It didn't make for very relaxed living.

Our living room led to a small dining room, and then straight back to the kitchen. Our parents' bedroom was downstairs, along with a small study. My dad spent an inordinate amount of time in the study "paying bills." Either we were in deep debt, or he was avoiding us on a regular basis. The only full bathroom was downstairs as well. The stairs were to the right of the living room, facing the front door.

Upstairs were Patty's and my little bedrooms, a hall closet with our mother's sewing machine, and a tiny bathroom with just a sink and toilet. Patty complained about this a lot because she hated using the downstairs bathroom for her marathon showers. One of our parents was always banging on the door telling her to get out of the bathroom. But our father said he would never put in a shower upstairs because he would go broke paying the water bill. I wanted to ask him if a higher water bill would add another day to his time in the study, but I didn't dare.

I peeked into the kitchen and saw my mother angrily tossing a salad, lettuce flying out of the bowl. Patty was sitting on the sacred couch in the living room, flipping through *Glamour* magazine. I didn't know how she could be so fearless within striking distance of our angry mother.

But then Patty made it her mission to thwart our mother every opportunity she got. She dyed her hair Marilyn Monroe blonde, which my mother considered "trashy." She wore tons of purple eye makeup and super short cut-offs, and bought a rabbit fur coat with babysitting money, which my mother declared only a streetwalker would wear.

When Patty wore the rabbit fur coat to Mass, our mother refused to sit with her. The irony was the rabbit fur shed all over everything, including all the other coats in the closet. Eventually, we were all wearing some rabbit fur. Many a dinnertime fight began with my parents providing a litany of my sister's wayward ways.

Tonight, for me, all signs pointed to lying low, so I grabbed my plant and card and scuttled upstairs to my bedroom to wait for dinner. I lay down on my bed, where I could see our backyard from one of my windows. I watched my dad grilling burgers, looking tired, hot, and miserable.

To the outside world, my parents were the picture of a solid marriage and a stable family. We lived in a respectable, if not affluent, neighborhood, went to Mass every Sunday, and were members of the school and church community. My father worked for the telephone company, and my mother raised two daughters and kept a lovely home and garden. Looking at my parents at Mass or school, you would never know our home was a war zone.

My dad, Thomas Daniel Murphy, was average height, trim, with a full head of hair at 42, and an easy smile. People often said he looked like Dean Martin, and the similarity extended to his love of cocktails. I generally got along well with my dad. When my mom wasn't there, he was pretty easy-going.

I occasionally watched baseball with him, and he taught me to play cards. Sometimes, he let me look through the telescope he had in his study, pointing out the constellations. As an avid fantasy reader, I was a bit obsessed with the stars and the Milky Way.

I also much preferred my dad attend any school events. Other people seemed to like him, and he didn't embarrass me. We weren't close but had an amiable relationship. He did most of the things a dad was supposed to do, and in turn, I didn't cause him any trouble.

Sometimes, my dad drank a lot. When he was drunk, he concentrated extra hard to do normal things, like walking or talking, as if he was wading through water. And often, after one of their epic fights, my father would play his records on the big stereo in his study and drink with the lights off. His favorite record was "Try to Remember" from a show he'd seen on Broadway once on a business trip. It was a sad song about lost youth and the passing of time, and my mother remarked on more than one occasion that my father was prone to melancholy because he was Irish. She was French and German, and apparently culturally immune to such bouts of sadness.

My dad had served in Korea, and I wondered if that had affected his disposition, but like most things, he never talked about the war. In many ways, my dad was a stranger living in our midst—generally courteous, occasionally explosive, but mostly elusive.

My mother, Vivian Reed Murphy, had been very pretty in her youth, according to her stories and the pictures she had on display on the mantle in the living room. She was still very attractive at 40. She was a bit tall, very thin, with piercing blue eyes, porcelain skin marked by only a few wrinkles around her eyes, and silky chestnut-brown hair she wore in a bun. Her clothes were conservative, but stylish and neat. My mother's appearance gave no hint of the deep unhappiness inside her.

My mother was the one in charge of the house, the family, the parenting, and if she had her way, the world. In her youth, my mother had seriously considered becoming a nun, and she ran our home like the mother superior of a very strict convent. Everything she looked at came under criticism: our house, the neighborhood, mostly my sister and me. I knew I was a constant disappointment to her. But my father was not immune from her criticism, and that's how the fights began. It always started with something small, over drinks, of course.

My parents' routine was to sit in the two wingback chairs in the living room and have cocktails with the evening newspaper. My mother drank scotch, and my dad had a Manhattan. Usually, my dad would start complaining about work, and my mother would—in her words—"play devil's advocate," which translated into telling him all the mistakes he made at his job.

My mother liked to call my dad an executive with the telephone company—and while it was true he wore a suit to work every day unlike most of our neighbors with blue-collar jobs—he wasn't a supervisor or boss. Once when she said it in front of Patty, Patty laughed, "Working in the accounting department hardly makes him an executive, Mom." For which she received a literal slap on the wrist.

My mother always wanted things to appear better than they actually were. She was immensely proud that our house was one of a handful of single-family houses in a street of duplexes. She had grown up in a duplex in a poorer part of town.

But she wasn't satisfied with our house in the city. She wanted to live in the suburbs. She was always picking up the free real estate brochures in the grocery store and leaving them by my dad's chair. My mom blamed my dad for being stuck in the city. She maintained if he was more competent at work, he could make more money, and we could move.

By the time dinner started many evenings, their eyes would be alive with alcohol and smoldering with anger. All it took was one match to start the blaze. My sister was often very happy to light that match.

That night, when we finally sat down to dinner, my parents were simply not speaking, which I felt was preferable to the screaming that could erupt at any minute. I sat mute and ate my burger. My sister, however, had a smirk on her face, and I worried what that meant.

"Well, Mom and Dad, I've made a decision," Patty announced, slapping her hands down on the Formica green table for emphasis and startling all of us from our thoughts. Then she paused for a moment, letting the tension build.

Watching my sister at dinner was a lot like watching a one-woman play. She was in the zone and commanded the room. She had starred in her fair share of drama productions at school.

"I've decided to do my junior and senior years at Milford Public," she grinned. Like I was, my sister was currently enrolled at Saint Christopher's, which conveniently had an elementary, middle, and high school. In reality, the schools were all housed in one building, but separate floors and halls served different grade levels. Saint Christopher's offered a K–12 Catholic education, so there was no escape from the nuns until college, and even then, my mother had her sights set on a Catholic college run by nuns, should we be worthy of attending college at all.

Patty knew that our parents were silently simmering, and I wondered why she got some perverse pleasure in reigniting the flame.

"You goddamn will not!" my father exploded. The veins in his head were bulging. I wanted to ask my father why his defense of Catholic education was littered with blasphemous expletives, but I knew better than to speak.

31

"Absolutely not!" my mother hissed. "Your father and I at least agree on this. You're enough of a problem as it is!" she declared, outraged at my sister, but still managing to get in a dig at my dad.

"It's a better school! And you aren't in charge of my life!" Patty screamed.

"We damn well are!" my father yelled back.

"The public school is better than that convent run by psycho nuns!" Patty screeched. Those were serious fighting words for my super Catholic parents.

On cue, I went around the house shutting the windows, despite the heat, so the neighbors wouldn't hear the battle. I rinsed my dish and put it in the dishwasher. I looked forlornly at my graduation cake still in the box on the counter, the frosting melting in the heat.

Then I went upstairs to my room to escape the chaos, snagging a couple of Twinkies on the way to celebrate myself alone. I probably could've taken the entire cake. No one seemed to notice anything I did when the fights started.

I knew Patty really wanted to change schools because the boy she liked went to the public school. And I further knew that my parents would hate him because I had seen him at the park talking with Patty and her friends. He had long hair, smoked, wore the same ratty Grateful Dead t-shirt every day it seemed, and was perpetually barefoot, all of which my mother would deem filthy habits.

A couple of weeks ago, the dinner fight began because Patty announced a plan to go to New York City with friends to see her favorite band, The Kinks. She shared this little trip idea over a dinner of fried chicken, reassuring our parents that it would be fine because her best friend Debbie's brother said they had a place to stay called the Port Authority, which, as it turned out, was a bus station.

My father had exploded so hysterically, the corn on the cob he had just chewed flew out of his mouth and landed grotesquely on my plate. I sat there looking at it, wondering if he would be offended if I got up and threw it out in my napkin. My mother asked Patty if she was planning to become a prostitute next and hang around bus stations looking for business. That fight had lasted a good, long time, and even featured a brief encore later in the evening, a couple hours after the main fight calmed down.

Pretty soon, I could hear all three of them downstairs screaming. Then I heard the front screen door slam, and I knew Patty had taken off. She couldn't go far. She only had the choice of her bike or her feet. But my sister loved a grand exit.

Of course, this didn't stop the fight. My parents turned on each other then, each blaming the other for Patty's rebellion. But it soon morphed into the familiar refrain of their unhappy marriage: my father called my mother cold and miserable, and said she was exactly like her mother. My mother said my father lacked ambition and drank too much, and we would never get out of this run-down house.

I avoided them and went about my nighttime routine. I brushed my teeth, washed my face, attempted to smooth my unruly mane, and then retreated back to the privacy of my room.

My room was small, but I liked it well enough. The walls were painted pale yellow, and my twin bed was soft and comfy. Last year with my birthday money, I purchased a fluffy comforter with hot pink, orange, and yellow flowers. My mother said it was garish, but I loved the bright colors.

I had a white desk and chair for homework and writing, and a bench by my street-side window to watch the world go by. My walls were decorated with pictures of Donny Osmond that I cut out of *Tiger Beat* magazine, along with David Cassidy, Bobby Sherman, and assorted other TV and pop stars.

I flipped on the radio, hoping my new favorite song would play— "Too Young," by Donny Osmond. I waited through a few songs, and when "Too Young" didn't come on, I turned off my radio.

I thought about playing a record. I loved "Alone Again Naturally," by Gilbert O'Sullivan, a sweet, sad little ditty about a man being jilted at the altar. However, my mother called the song maudlin and changed the station every time it came on in the car. The last thing I wanted to do tonight was incur her wrath.

Instead, I wrote in my journal for a while and munched on the Twinkies. I wanted to be a professional writer when I grew up, so I made myself write a little bit every day. Where my sister's role in the family was instigator, mine was watcher. I was a keen observer of everything around me. And I often wrote my observations in my journals, marble school notebooks that I hid in a Madame Alexander doll box under my bed. I didn't want my mother to discover what her life looked like through her youngest daughter's eyes.

Sometimes I wrote about what I saw looking outside my window instead. When the fighting was happening, it calmed me to look out my window onto the street below and watch my neighbors doing normal things: weeding gardens, mowing lawns, chatting on the sidewalk, pushing babies in strollers.

I imagined conversations and made them into characters for stories I would write, jotting down small details, facial expressions, laughter, or the way some neighbors studiously avoided talking to anyone. I loved to examine the small details other people never noticed.

There wasn't much happening in the neighborhood tonight, just old Mr. Feeney raking his lawn and talking to himself, and Mrs. Johnson sitting on her front porch with a cup of tea or coffee, watching the street. I jotted down those details, along with a run-down of tonight's main event, and then tucked my journal back in the box under my bed.

I decided to read for a while until I felt sleepy. I was reading the fantasy book called *A Wizard of Earthsea* by Ursula K. Le Guin, about a boy named Ged who learns he is a gifted wizard. I loved reading fantasy books, dreaming of a world in which I could be powerful and magical. My favorite books of all time were *The Chronicles of Narnia*. When I was younger, I would walk in my closet, pretending it was an enchanted wardrobe where I could escape to a magical world. Reading was a joy and an escape for me, and English was the one class in which I always earned good grades.

I read for a while, and finally, when I was tired enough, I turned off my light. I knew my parents wouldn't come upstairs to say goodnight, and there was no way I was going downstairs to them when they were likely sulking in separate corners of the house. I was relieved, if a bit lonely, that I didn't hear either one of them climbing the stairs.

A couple hours after she made her defiant exit, I heard Patty come up the stairs and shut her door, and I assumed she was staring at her pores in her light-up makeup mirror, as was her nightly ritual. The makeup mirror had three settings: day, evening, and nightclub. Every night, Patty would make faces, experiment with makeup, and examine her pores in each setting.

Patty was far prettier than I would ever be. She was thin and had long, wavy, light-brown hair. Her eyes were blue, whereas mine were brown. I never thought anything of that until Grandma held my face in her hands when I was about eight, and said, "Shame you didn't get Patty's blue eyes. Yours are mud brown." It was one of the many times Grandma found me pitiable and hurt my feelings with such a blunt observation about my appearance. My list of grievances against Grandma grew longer every day.

My nighttime ritual wasn't as carefree as Patty's. I had been afraid of the dark ever since I was little, and age was not remedying it. Superstitiously, I arranged my baby dolls and stuffed animals around me for protection.

Patty and I had played baby dolls for years, giving each doll a distinct and often comically hostile personality. That was Patty's touch. Even though Patty rarely humored me anymore with doll voices, I still felt my dolls were alive in a way, and my sentinels watching over me at night. I blessed myself, then flopped on my stomach and crossed my hands under me. Then I said my prayers until I fell asleep.

The familiar nightmare returned. I was lying on my back, like a turtle without a shell, and a vampire flew down on top of me. I scrambled to my feet only to find myself in the fruit cellar of my grandparents' house. I could feel its dirt walls around me. Then I saw the single lightbulb that hung from the ceiling illuminating my grandfather's face. I woke up suddenly, startled. It was 3 am.

I had been having this same dream for years. I almost told Gina once, but I was afraid of what she would think of me. I was pretty sure if I told Gina about the dream, she would figure it all out. Gina was sharp about stuff like that.

I got out of bed to make sure I was fully awake, so I wouldn't fall asleep and start the nightmare again. I sat on the bench by my window and looked out on my neighborhood. It was a dark moonless night, with only streetlights blinking stingy light into the street.

I could see someone walking quickly down the street—a man. I couldn't tell who he was, but he was looking around him as he hurried. He disappeared around the corner, and I couldn't decide if he was real or if I had dreamed him up. He was more shadow than person.

Finally, with my light on, I fell back into a dreamless sleep.

Lingering Clouds
Saturday, June 24, 1972

The next morning, I woke and bolted downstairs to watch my cartoons—*Sabrina, the Teenage Witch* was my favorite because it was a spin-off of *The Archies*, my beloved comic. But there was a new *Osmond Brothers* cartoon, and a *Jackson Five* cartoon, followed by *American Bandstand* and *Soul Train*.

Saturday morning TV was pure gold. I poured a hefty bowl of Cocoa Puffs and plopped myself on the rug, right in front of the TV. But halfway through *Sabrina*, my mom walked in and turned the TV off. I was devastated, but my sad face did not even put a dent in her icy mood.

"We have a lot of cleaning to do today," she announced with a huff.

I looked around for my sister and my dad, but they were scarce.

"Where are Patty and Dad?" I asked, hoping Patty could start the cleaning without me, and I could turn the TV back on.

"Your father is in his study, and your sister has apparently taken it upon herself to go out for the day," she reported angrily. If Patty wasn't here, I guess I was the target for her anger. And if she couldn't control Patty, she was going to make it clear, I was still under her thumb.

She pulled the old ten-ton Kirby vacuum out of the front hall closet and shoved it in front of me.

"But, Mom, I wait all week for my shows," I whined and remained sitting on the floor.

"Cartoons are for children, and you are about to be in middle school. Besides, vacuuming will give you some exercise and you can work off that giant bowl of cereal," she stared down at me and looked with disgust at the chocolaty milk left in my cereal bowl. Humiliation enveloped me. Shaming was a special talent of hers. She whipped around and headed for the kitchen.

"Where do you want me to vacuum?" I asked with a sigh.

My mother turned to face me; her blue eyes steely. "Everywhere," she waved her hand around to indicate the wide scope of the cleaning and walked briskly into the kitchen, the door flapping in anger behind her. I could hear her slamming cabinets. It was that kind of day. Plus, it was raining, so I couldn't escape on my bike to Richie's house.

I dragged the vacuum cord to the outlet and began to push the vacuum around, its noisy engine buffering the world around me. I daydreamed about Charlie and better days ahead.

The rest of the day passed in a blur of tedious chores. I tried calling Richie once, but the line was busy. With six people in their house, their phone was often tied up.

Eventually my sister arrived home, but she went straight to her room. My father barely came out of the den all day, lots of bills to pay apparently. Dinner was a silent meal of meatloaf and potatoes. No one had an appetite for conversation and barely any for the food.

I hated my mom's meatloaf because she put big chunks of onions and peppers in it, and I spent most of the meal picking them out of my slice. I saw my mother glance at the pile of discarded onions and peppers on the side of my plate, and she shot me a look, but she didn't break the silence at the table.

After dinner, Patty and I watched TV together. Saturday night TV in summer was all reruns, so we watched an old movie, *The Creature from the Black Lagoon*. Patty thought it was funny because it was so ridiculous, but I found it scary. At points in the movie, the monster would swim right under the girl in the murky lagoon, and she had no idea he was there. Watching the creature stalk and lurk around the girl gave me chills.

Finally, the morose day came to an end, and Patty and I trudged upstairs to bed. After I brushed my teeth in our small bathroom, I went to my sister's room. Patty's room was all pink. Pink comforter, pink chair cushion, pink rug. But she also had lots of posters of the Kinks, the Beatles, the Who, and other assorted rock bands my mother found offensive.

For a while, Patty wanted to become a singer. Many times, I had been a literal captive audience as she stood on a kitchen chair and sang "Son of a Preacher Man" using a hairbrush as a microphone. Patty knew that song irritated my mother with its tale of illicit sex with a traveling preacher's son.

I tried to find a place to sit on Patty's bed, but as usual there were piles of clothes tossed everywhere. Patty changed her clothes about ten times a day, and she didn't put any of them away because in her words, "she would wear them eventually." A Kinks record was playing a song called "Sunny Afternoon." Patty had a nicer record player than I did, but her albums were always piled on top of each other, out of their jackets, and often if I borrowed one, I'd find make-up on it. She called her room an organized mess, but it was just a mess.

"Patty, do you think Mom and Dad will get a divorce?" I asked for her teenage wisdom. She laughed. Then she pushed her clothes pile aside and motioned for me to sit down.

"No, they're too Catholic. They will just make each other miserable until they're dead," she said with a bitter laugh.

"Sometimes I wish they would, and I would live with Dad," I confessed and looked at the ground.

"Mags, they are not getting divorced. Vivian would be mortified," Patty exaggerated our mother's name when she spoke, putting her hand to her forehead, miming our mother fainting in humiliation. Sometimes, Patty casually attempted to address our parents by their first names in conversation, and it always provoked the irrational fury from them she was seeking. To my mother, Patty calling her Vivian was tantamount to blasphemy.

"Yeah, I guess you're right," I agreed with Patty's assessment and sighed.

"And if they ever did, we would totally have to live with Viv. So, don't wish that. Just know that in a few years, you can be outta here. That's my plan. I mean I love them in a way, I guess. They're our parents, but Vivian's a class A bitch, and Tom's practically an alcoholic. They are completely insane," she explained as she began her evening ritual of brushing her hair in front of her make-up mirror.

"Do you really think that?" I asked her, startled at her brash assessment of our parents.

"Don't you?" she asked with a laugh. Then seeing my dismayed face, she tried to console me with some Patty wisdom, "Chill out. Everyone has a messed-up family."

"Not Richie. His family is amazing," I replied with envy in my voice.

Patty sat still for a minute and then turned to face me.

"Well, then you can have that kind of family when you grow up. But for now, we are stuck with this insanity," Patty said flatly and crossed her eyes for comic effect.

As I said my prayers that night, I wasn't sure what to pray for. I just asked God to make something in my life change.

Mass on Sundays

Sunday, June 25, 1972

Despite a Saturday of marital cold war, Sunday morning was still Mass. Not a family battle nor natural disaster could keep us from church on a Sunday morning.

As usual, we got dressed in a rush and piled into my dad's green Dodge Coronet. My parents made small talk about the weather, which was the first I heard my dad speak in a full 24 hours. Patty stared sourly out the window. I saw my mother look back at her and glare at Patty's full face of makeup, but for once she didn't say anything.

I think Patty put on extra makeup for church just to embarrass our mother, who apparently felt everyone was scrutinizing our family during our walk to communion, which probably said more about what my mother did during Mass than anything else.

Saint Christopher's Church was part of my school, so attending Mass on Sundays was just another chance to see the same kids who didn't talk to me in school. One of the families on our street was Presbyterian, and they apparently took the summers off from church. I asked my mother once if we could do that, and she snipped at me that God didn't mention anything in the Bible about summer vacation.

Father Anthony was giving the sermon, and I tried to pay attention, but he was boring. He was assigned to our parish last year as an assistant pastor to Father Hurley, our regular pastor. Father Anthony was assigned the job of youth pastor, so he was in school a lot. The nuns introduced him as Father Mancuso, but he told us to all call him Father Anthony, I guess in some attempt to be less intimidating. But he still had the collar and giant cross around his neck, so it didn't really work. Plus, he was a scrawny, nervous man, with a pock-marked complexion. As much as he wanted to be the fun, hip young priest, he always seemed kind of awkward and pitiful.

Father Anthony wasn't super popular with my classmates, and one boy in my class, Timmy Constantine, hated him. Timmy had been an altar boy before Father Anthony arrived, but he quit soon after. My mother said Timmy had a bad temper and was headed for trouble. I asked Timmy once why he hated Father Anthony, but all he said was Father Anthony was a loser.

I had no real opinion about Father Anthony because he had never really said anything to me. I would just see him kind of wandering the playground or lingering in the back of classrooms. It was kind of unnerving how sometimes he would suddenly be standing right behind you, and you hadn't realized it. Some of the kids called him The Holy Ghost because he moved so quietly and just kind of hovered.

The sermon droned on, followed by the same old hymns and prayers I could say in my sleep. There were big fans blowing on the altar, but it was still hot in church.

During communion, I spied my third-grade teacher Sister Marguerite in the back of the church. She smiled at me, and I avoided eye contact. Sister Marguerite had once convinced my mother that I should attend a day retreat at a local convent, where I ate sloppy Joes and stale potato chips while watching filmstrips about Jesus and vocations.

Patty was certain the retreat invite meant that Sister Marguerite had identified me as nun material, and I was now paranoid whenever she was nice to me. Nuns had frightening mind control powers. A girl Patty and I grew up with, Theresa Malone, who seemed perfectly normal for 16 years, had recently entered the convent after spending time with Sister Marguerite.

What I really wished was that I had the nerve to march back there and tell her I would never be a nun, so she could keep her smile. She'd lost my affection years ago anyway with her Nativity Play fix.

Every year Sister Marguerite picked a pretty girl to be Mary in the Nativity Play. Jessica got the role twice! After years of being an anonymous angel, I asked her if I could finally have a real part. She said yes with a quizzical look that told me it had never occurred to her to put me in the actual action of the play.

But instead of finally getting the coveted role of Mary, she cast me as the innkeeper who tells Joseph and Mary there is no room for them and sends them off into the cold night. Apparently, I was best suited to be the villain in the Nativity Play, so I sure as heck wasn't nun material. I complained to my mother about this, but only received a stiff scolding. I should have known better. In the world of my parents, the nuns, and the Church, adults were always right, and kids were not to question their often mysterious and frustrating ways.

After church, we piled back in the family car for the ritual Sunday trip to Grandma's. My grandma, Edna Reed, lived a short drive from our house and church, and we went there weekly to eat stale coffee cake and visit with her. Grandma preferred Saturday afternoon Mass, "less rush," she claimed, although I never thought of church as fast-moving.

My mother's older brother, our Uncle Jimmy, lived with Grandma, despite being in his 40's. He was a bachelor, according to my mother, as if he was single by choice. But I just thought he was fat and miserable, and no woman in her right mind would want anything to do with him.

Uncle Jimmy was one of the custodians at Milford Public High School, and my mother always referred to him as the head of maintenance, which was not his job title. My dad would scoff when she called Uncle Jimmy that; he'd remark how amazing it was that a guy who has such bad asthma that he couldn't fight in Korea had no problem spending his day sweeping up dirt and chalk dust.

Grandma had a two-family house, and she lived in one half with Uncle Jimmy, and another old lady lived in the other half. She was our only living grandparent. My father's parents had died a year apart after he returned home from Korea, so Patty and I had never met them. And my mother's father died two years ago. Mom was always telling us that we were fortunate to still have Grandma, but I never felt particularly lucky in her presence.

We arrived, and after stiff hugs from Grandma, my sister and I got coffee cake and juice, and sat on the front steps. We never liked to sit inside her house because it had a musty smell that I attributed to Uncle Jimmy, although Patty said it was just because they never opened their windows. Uncle Jimmy was of the dimwitted belief that the house would stay cooler in the summer if the windows stayed shut. But all it did was keep the hot, smelly air inside.

Patty and I sat in silence for a while and watched a bunch of boys playing basketball in the driveway of a house across the street. Grandma's neighborhood was a more interesting mixture of people than ours. Her neighbors across the street on one side were Black, and down the street there was a family of Hasidic Jews, and the men had those long curls in front and wore the all-black suits. Patty told me their curls were attached to their hats, and I believed her until one day, I saw the man mowing his lawn in the heat. He took his hat off to fan his face, and the tendrils stayed on his head. It was neither the first nor last time my sister fed me absurd misinformation for her own amusement. Yet I always believed her.

My mother often remarked that the neighborhood had gone downhill in the years since she lived there. But to me, it looked exactly like our neighborhood except that everyone on our street was white.

I could hear my mother and grandmother talking about me through the screen door. I wondered if they wanted me to hear them.

"All she wants to do is spend time with Richie. I let it go when they were little kids, but she's growing up now and it's not acceptable," my mother carped at Grandma. I sighed, thinking how I was always a problem to her.

"Well, it's not like he's a regular boy. You don't have to worry there. But she does need girlfriends. I hate to say this, Vivian, but Margaret Grace is downright odd," Grandma stated worriedly.

Patty heard them too and started talking to drown out their voices.

"Are you and Richie still roller-skating?" she asked me.

"Yeah," I replied flatly.

I could tell she was feeling sorry for me, but I was still a bit suspect when Patty was kind to me. The sting of Patty's wretched adolescent years lingered. As children, we had always gotten along despite our four-year age difference. But as soon as Patty hit 12, she became impossible. She hated everything and everyone, especially her family. As she navigated the misery of adolescence, I had been the easiest target for her teasing and criticism.

One summer when she was 13 and I was 9, she started calling me "the fatted calf." She stumbled on the Biblically cruel insult at Mass one week and it stuck for two months. For my own safety and sanity, we had drifted apart.

But that spring she had turned sixteen, and she seemed to be softening towards me. She would never apologize for calling me chubs or her weirdo little sister, but sometimes I thought I saw regret in her eyes, so I easily forgave her. She was my only sibling.

"What does she mean Richie isn't a regular boy?" I asked, and Patty stretched out her long legs on the steps and looked at the sky, searching for an answer.

"Is it because he's Black? Cause that's wrong!" I asserted, suddenly defiant and angry.

"It's because he likes to play dolls and dance with you. He doesn't play with other boys," Patty stated bluntly.

45

"So? That's what he likes, and what I like." I felt tears forming in my eyes. Why was I always made to feel that everything about me was wrong? If I was odd, it wasn't on purpose.

Patty turned to face me; her expression serious.

"Listen, Mags, they are two mean old crones, mom and Grandma. Just try to find a few school friends too. You don't have to stop being friends with Richie. Besides, if you don't see Richie, I will never see Charlie, and he's a god!" she smiled. There was no cute guy on Earth who escaped my sister's notice.

"Okay, but I'm marrying Charlie. I called him first," I reminded her.

"That's not exactly how that works," she laughed.

Patty then entertained me with a story about a boy her friend Debbie liked, and how Debbie was stalking the kid as he walked to work, so she could just "happen" to run into him. Now the boy was walking an entirely different route to avoid her.

My mother and grandmother were now talking to my dad about the gutters at Grandma's house, so I felt safe enough to go inside. I had to use the bathroom.

"Use the upstairs one, Maggie," Grandma called as I walked past them in her boiling living room. "Uncle Jimmy is in the downstairs bathroom."

Uncle Jimmy practically lived in the bathroom, at least when we were over. But his room was upstairs, so I don't know why he was holed up in the downstairs bathroom. I hated going upstairs, and I especially hated the upstairs bathroom. I couldn't hold it though, and the last thing I needed to do was pee my pants at 12. That would be the final piece of evidence to condemn me as a loser.

"Go ahead, Kiddo," my dad said as I passed, and he patted my back. He must have heard my mother and Grandma talking about what a loser I was and felt bad for me.

I walked up the narrow, dark stairs quickly, trying to calm the panic that always rose in me when I had to go upstairs at Grandma's house.

Nothing could hurt me now, I knew that in my mind, but my body still panicked.

I went into the small bathroom with the cracked subway tile, but I couldn't bring myself to shut the door. I looked at the water meter, and felt my throat tighten. I could see that the hole my grandfather had drilled in the bathroom wall was still there. I used to plug it up with toilet paper out of the fear of seeing an eye looking through at me.

On the other side of the bathroom wall was a closet where Grandpa kept his work clothes. I mentioned the hole once to Grandma, but she just mumbled something about mice and getting an exterminator. I was pretty sure the kind of exterminator Grandma needed didn't get rid of mice.

I peed as quickly as I could, flushed, and ran back down the stairs without even stopping to wash my hands. I had to get out of there. I was panting when I reached the living room.

My mother just stared at me as if I was an alien. But she was the last person I could explain anything to.

On the way home in the car, I asked my mother why we had to go there every Sunday.

Without turning around, she scolded me, "Because your grandmother has been lonely since Grandpa died, and she looks forward to seeing her family."

My sister stared at my mother expressionless. And I asked God to forgive me for being glad my grandfather was dead.

Charlie

Monday, June 26, 1972

The next day was the official start of summer vacation. Patty and I had English muffins with grape jelly for breakfast, and she even made me a cup of coffee. It was bitter, but I wanted to like it, so I poured a ton of sugar in it, and Patty smirked and rolled her eyes at me.

Mom was in her garden, where she spent much of her time. She seemed to enjoy her plants more than her family, and I often wondered if she was cultivating herbs to use in some kind of magic potion to transform all of us into people she might actually like.

After breakfast, Patty took off on her bike to see friends, and I was sitting on the bottom step of the stairs by the living room, putting my sneakers on, about to head to Richie's house, when I heard the back screen door open and close. My mother walked into the living room.

"Maggie, I'd like to speak to you," she announced.

I walked into the room hesitantly, and she motioned for me to sit next to her on the fancy floral sofa, a piece of furniture usually forbidden to me. She sat first and waited. As I perched gingerly on the edge of the cushion, she stared at me, and I wondered what horrible misdeed I had committed to warrant this talk.

"Where are you going, Maggie?" she asked with a frozen smile, although it was clearly an interrogation.

"Outside to play," I offered vaguely, feeling uncomfortable as I always did when conversing with my mother and not wanting to have the conversation about my lack of acceptable friends.

"With Richie?" she pressed me for details.

"Well, yeah, I figured I would head over there and see what's up," I trailed off and started picking at a hangnail I had been working on.

"Maggie, you know I like Richie, and I am not prejudiced in any way. I was raised better than that. But you are nearly a teenager, and it's simply not appropriate for your best friend to be a boy," she explained firmly.

I stared at the China cabinet and sighed deeply.

"You need to find girlfriends your own age. You need girls to learn how to be sociable; you need role models," she tried to explain this gaping hole in my development.

"I have you and Patty as role models," I countered her, hoping the compliment would shut her down.

"That's not enough. Girlfriends talk about clothes and hair, and they help you figure out how to be in the world. Don't you want that?" She questioned me, and I saw her take in my frizzy ponytail and supremely unfashionable t-shirt and shorts. I wanted to mention that she had chosen my wardrobe, but I didn't dare.

It was true I didn't try as hard as I should with my appearance, but that was only because when I did, it never worked out, and my futile attempts at fashion were too painful. My graduation dress was still in a ball on the floor of my closet, mocking me for my attempt to be pretty.

I let out a sigh and searched for any words to say to my mother, but as so often was the case, she asked questions like the Sphinx, and I felt like jumping off a cliff.

She stared at me for a minute, and I just shrugged which seemed to infuriate her.

"Why don't you have friends?" she asked, her hands palms upward in exasperation.

It was far beyond me to explain to my mother that I was a social misfit, that I had always been shy, that once I found Richie, I was so happy, I stopped looking for other people. How could I explain that other girls were mean, and I had bad hair, and no fashion sense, and that Richie accepted me just as I was?

I couldn't tell her that I loved being with his family, that everyone there was warm and laughed, and his parents hugged and kissed. It would all make her furious.

My mother was nothing like me. She had been on the prom court in high school and had dated a basketball player, who was now some big banker in New York, and whose name she liked to trot out occasionally to make my father feel inadequate.

So, I stayed quiet and waited for her to dismiss me. We sat in silence for a bit before she sighed deeply with disappointment and said, "Be home for supper."

I ran out the door while the running was good. I scurried to the side of the house, hopped on my beautiful, yellow banana-seat bike with the floral basket, and began to pedal the five-minute ride to Richie's house.

As much as I tried to dismiss my mother's words, they still stung. What was wrong with me? How could a mother and daughter be so completely different? Was I adopted? Was that why she looked at me like I was some refugee washed up on her shore?

I passed our neighbor, Mr. Feeney, as I turned the corner. Mr. Feeney was in his seventies, all bent over and frail. His legs and arms were scrawny, but his belly was round. His hair hovered over his bony scalp in scraggly wisps. He bore a striking resemblance to the little plastic troll doll I won as a prize at the Church Carnival last winter in the Fish Toss Game. Father Anthony was running the game, and when he handed the doll to me, my first thought was that someone had created a pint-sized rendering of Mr. Feeney.

Mr. Feeney usually had something mean to say to kids who ventured near his house. He was a widower, and his only child, a son, had been killed in Vietnam eight years ago. He spent most of his time writing angry letters to the newspaper and yelling at neighborhood kids playing in the road.

Mr. Feeney didn't like Gina because she had protested the war, and he saved some of his meanest tirades for her, but she always just smiled and waved in return. My mother said he was tragic, but it was hard to feel sorry for him when he was so nasty.

When I passed, Mr. Feeney was watering his lawn, despite the fact that it was yellow and brown and looked as if it would never grow again. Out of politeness, I smiled and waved at him. He ignored me, and I counted myself lucky.

I turned the corner to head to Richie's house. As I pedaled my bike closer, I could feel my worries shrink and my smile grow. It meant the world to me to have another family. I knew I wasn't really a member of the Harper family, but I could pretend I was when I was there, and that was enough. And if my life unfolded as I dreamed, I would one day be Charlie's wife and a bona fide Harper.

I arrived at Richie's house and was thrilled to see Charlie's green Chevelle parked in front. My heart always did a little leap when I knew he was home. No matter how many times I saw Charlie, it was like seeing a movie star in person.

Charlie was coming down the front steps with Gina as I got off my bike. Gina and Charlie had been close friends since elementary school. Lots of people in town thought they were dating because they had gone to the Senior Prom together, but Gina assured me they were simply good friends. Of course, the sight of a white girl and a Black boy at the prom together had whipped the town gossips into a cyclone of conjecture at the time.

My mother's best friend, Mrs. Conway, had lots to say on the subject of Gina's and Charlie's friendship. On many a bridge night my mother hosted, I overheard Mrs. Conway decrying Gina as wild and "provocative." "Provocative" was one of Mrs. Conway's favorite words as far as I could tell, and she liberally assigned it to people, television shows, and politicians.

51

But Gina never let anyone's opinion change hers. She remained calm and ignored the stares and criticism of other people, whether it was Mr. Feeney or Mrs. Conway. Gina said she and Charlie had a great time at the prom, and she highly recommended him as a prom date, which, of course, got me thinking of ways to coerce him into taking me to my prom when the time came.

Gina had been babysitting since graduating last year, and Charlie had been working at his dad's garage, but this summer they were starting classes at the community college together.

"Hey Maggie May!" Gina smiled a hello, always happy to see me.

"It's Snow White," Charlie grinned at me, and I could feel myself melting on the sidewalk. He had been calling me that for years, telling me I looked like the Disney princess because of my dark hair and fair skin. Charlie was the one person who made me feel like I actually had a shot at being pretty one day.

He looked especially dreamy today in his blue jeans and a black t-shirt, red Converse All Stars on his feet. I could see his muscles, and as usual, his smile made me dizzy.

Gina looked as beautiful as always in a peasant dress and sandals, her long hair loose and silky. How I wished for hair like that. It struck me then that with her olive skin so tan, she and Charlie had practically the same skin tone, and I thought how bizarre it was that they were considered different races.

"Where are you guys going?" I asked, still sitting on my bike.

"We are going to our first summer class. Child Psychology," she informed me.

"Maybe we could just study you and Richie," Charlie nudged me, and I felt my cheeks burning red. My heart sank. I didn't want him to think of me as a child.

"How was the party, Gina? Were lots of interesting people there?" I asked brightly, trying to sound sophisticated. I thought maybe if I seemed up to date on her social life, I would seem more like a peer and less like a child. I was desperate to impress Charlie.

She and Charlie exchanged looks and smirks.

"Well, it wasn't a great night. Ray and I broke up," she said gently, as if I would be disappointed. I mean he was cute, but he had never been particularly nice to me. I noticed she had on a new necklace that spelled Evangelina in gold letters. It glittered in the sunshine. I almost felt bad for Ray; he got dumped after finally buying Gina a nice present. For Christmas last year, he had gotten her a bike pump.

Suddenly, Richie came bounding down the front steps, "Maggie!!!" He was wearing his favorite orange t-shirt and gym shorts. And of course, he was barefoot.

"I've got the best dance for us! And Grandma Rose bought me the record!" he hollered and immediately started dancing on the sidewalk. Richie's level of excitement for things was always off the charts.

Charlie and Gina just laughed.

"Don't hurt yourself, Richie!" Charlie teased Richie as he spun around to a song only he could hear.

"When can we hang out, Gina?" I asked, trying to lower my voice, which always sounded squeaky in Charlie's presence.

Gina tilted her head and smiled.

"I've got an idea. I don't have to work tomorrow. How about a picnic at Orchard Beach? I'll bring the food and you bring the fun. You too, Richie," she added and poked him in the stomach.

"Sounds great," I beamed. I decided to be brave and ask Charlie to come.

"How about you, Charlie? Can you come to our beach picnic?" I asked hopefully, as he stood there, jingling his car keys.

He looked at Gina and asked with false formality, his hand on his chest, "A picnic? Am I invited to this social event?"

"You're kind of required to be there because you are my ride," she smirked. I had a moment of panic, realizing that Gina was now available to date Charlie. Was she flirting?

"Then, I'm in," he bowed and smiled that blinding smile. Gina and Charlie walked toward his car, and then she turned back to me.

"Maggie, you should invite Patty," she reminded me.

"Okay, but she might be too cool to attend." I air-quoted "too cool," and both Gina and Charlie laughed.

"Can you and Patty ride your bikes or is it too far?" Gina asked. She still worried about us as if we were little kids.

"It's fine. We can ride," I reassured her. It was far, but it was worth it.

"Okay, then we can meet around noon?" Gina asked.

"We will be there!" I promised.

"Goodbye, Maggie May and Little Richard," Gina waved and blew a kiss.

"See you tomorrow, Maggie," Charlie said, and my heart fluttered a bit.

"Have fun," I said, realizing how stupid it sounded as soon as it came out. They were headed to school after all. I always sounded so moronic in front of Charlie. He scrambled my brain.

Then they took off in Charlie's car, and I watched until the car turned the corner and was out of sight. I was smiling so hard it hurt. Richie looked at me.

"Oh, man, you are so in love with Charlie," he teased.

"Shut up. I am not. I just really like and respect him," I replied, feeling my cheeks burning up. Then I punched his arm for emphasis. He just laughed at me.

Family Dinner

Richie and I spent the rest of the afternoon in his garage practicing a dance to "Ooh Child," by the Five Stair Steps. I tried my best to keep up with his choreography, but I was no match for him. We laughed so hard at times, I had to sit on the concrete floor. But Richie's energy was boundless. After a while, we went into the house, and Grandma Rose had lemonade and my graduation cake waiting for us.

Like our house, Richie's was a foursquare style with roughly the same layout, except the room we used as a den was Richie's and Charlie's room. Our house had nicer furniture and was generally spotless. But even though Richie's house was older and more worn-out than ours, I liked it better. The Harpers' house always smelled like good food cooking and his grandma's perfume, and it was just so cozy and comfortable.

I never worried I was going to spill on the couch and make someone mad. And there was always a deck of cards on the dining room table because Grandma Rose liked to play. We were free to sit there, drinking lemonade and talking to her. Nothing was formal or off-limits. Richie's family liked me and seemed happy to see me when I was there. At home, it was like I was always holding my breath, but at Richie's house I could exhale.

"So, Maggie, what are you planning to do this summer?" Grandma Rose asked me, giving me a big hug with her question as I ate the amazing buttercream frosting on her homemade cake.

"I'm not sure. I guess dance, and write, and hang out with Richie," I offered meekly, a bit nervous since my plans were never well-received by my own family.

"Sounds like a grand plan," she smiled. "And hopefully, you will continue to sample my baking. I have some new recipes I want to try," she winked at me.

"Oh, Maggie will eat your cakes, Grandma," Richie teased me, and I punched him lightly in the arm for the second time that day. I know he didn't say it to be mean, but I didn't appreciate jokes about my weight. I got quiet. Grandma Rose noticed.

"Something wrong, Maggie?" she asked gently.

"I just know I'm fat, and I shouldn't eat so much dessert," I confessed with a sigh and crossed my arms over my stomach to hide my girth.

"Maggie, I think you're a beautiful girl. You don't need to change a thing about you," she soothed me with her kind words, words I would never hear at home.

"Just like I tell my Richie. God doesn't make mistakes. Everyone is perfect just the way God made them," Grandma Rose smiled at both of us and engulfed us in a warm, lovely hug.

After our snack, Richie and I sat out on the front steps and just talked for a while.

"I'm pretty surprised Gina dumped Ray," I shared. "They have been dating for like *two* years," I said, emphasizing the two because it seemed an eternity to me.

"Yeah, I guess. Did you really like him?" Richie asked.

"Not that much, but still," I drifted off, not sure what to say.

"Aw, they probably just had a fight," Richie suggested.

"Yeah, they will probably get back together tomorrow," I predicted.

As much as I wasn't crazy about Ray, I was selfishly worried that Gina and Charlie might get together. I loved Gina, but I didn't want her to have Charlie. I wanted him to wait for me.

"Did you watch *Bandstand* and *Soul Train* this week?" he asked me, his foot tapping on the step to imaginary music even as we sat there. Sitting still was not something Richie could do, and I knew he had gotten in trouble in school more than once for his high energy.

"I missed it. My mom made me clean," I complained to him.

"Man, Maggie, your mom is tough," he sympathized. It was always such a relief to hear someone acknowledge that my mother was not an easy person.

"Well, they had new dancers on *Soul Train* this week, and they were amazing. I can't wait to move to California or New York and become a real choreographer. I bet I could get on *Soul Train* if I was in California," he mused. I was sure he could.

"You definitely could, but I couldn't get on either show," I replied, and we both laughed. As much as I tried to dance, I was not coordinated at all. I was 100% effort and zero skill.

"Well, that's okay because you are going to be my agent, or my manager, while you start your writing career. And we are going to get a really cool apartment, with one of those sunken living rooms and lots of mirrors. And if it's in California, we will be on the beach, or if it's New York, we will be able to see the Empire State Building," he was dreaming aloud, and I was right there with him.

In my version of the dream, I was tall and thin, and my hair was like silk. Charlie would come to visit us and fall instantly in love with the new sophisticated me. I never questioned why Richie and I would always be friends, never romantic with each other. Our relationship was not like that. We were brother and sister, just like our dolls. Mean people insinuated things about Richie; they said he wasn't a normal boy. But I didn't care. Whoever he was now or would be in the future, Richie would always be my best friend.

Richie didn't share his dream about being a dancer or choreographer with anyone but me, not even his grandma. As much as his parents loved him, I knew they worried about him. After the baseball thing didn't work out, his father tried to get him to play basketball at the YMCA. Richie was good at that too, despite his puny size. But again, his heart wasn't in it. He would rather hang out with me, practicing our dances in the garage.

We had endured a lot of teasing about it from neighborhood kids over the years, especially my Catholic school classmates on my street. They called Richie a sissy and asked me if I was "colored" because my hair was so frizzy. They said we should get married because we were both losers and no one else would ever want us. I worried in my heart that there was truth in their words. Mostly, we ignored them; however, sometimes after a round of name-calling, I would see tears on Richie's cheeks, but he would never talk about it.

Mr. Harper's car pulled into the driveway, and he waved to us on the front porch. A few minutes later, Richie's Grandma called him to dinner through the front screen door.

"Can Maggie eat with us?" he asked. "She doesn't have to be home for like another hour."

I felt my cheeks burn with embarrassment because my mother would have grimaced at a last-minute dinner invitation.

"Sure, as long as she likes tacos," Grandma Rose smiled at me.

"I never had tacos," I answered, intrigued. I didn't have to be home because we ate later than everyone else so my parents could have their cocktail hour. Maybe I would like tacos.

"What?" Richie howled. "Tacos are the best!" he yelled and pulled me inside the house.

Normally, eating at someone else's house would have made me nervous, but from the very first time Richie brought me home and introduced me as his best friend, his parents had always made me feel as if I belonged there.

Mr. and Mrs. Harper were very different from my own parents, and spending time with them made me believe that marriage and family could be happy things.

Richie's mom, Maria, was a nurse and always seemed calm and content. She was an expert at soothing cuts, applying Band-Aids, and generously giving hugs.

His dad, Big Richie, was a mechanic who ran a local garage. He was a huge man and had even briefly played professional football. He had the biggest hands I'd ever seen, but his smile was just as big, and he laughed easily.

When Mr. Harper sat down at the dinner table, he kissed his wife on the lips, and I had to try not to stare because I had never seen such affection between my own parents.

The house smelled like cheese and spice, and when we sat at the table together, everyone was laughing and talking. I wished Charlie would get home, but I supposed he was still off somewhere with Gina.

"Let's say 'Grace'," Mr. Harper said, and I automatically blessed myself and started the Catholic prayer. I got embarrassed when everyone looked at me.

"Go ahead and say your prayer," Mr. Harper motioned to me with a smile. I mumbled my prayer. Then Mr. Harper spoke casually to God.

"Thank you, Lord, for our meal, and for family, and for our wonderful friend Maggie who's joining us tonight to have tacos for the first time," he smiled at me.

The tacos were amazing, and I ate three. Dinner was a happy event in Richie's house, and mostly Richie entertained everyone by doing impersonations of his dad and Charlie.

Toward the end of the meal, Richie's sister Monica arrived home from the library. She greeted me with a smile and a hug.

Monica was one year older than my sister Patty. Monica was petite with beautiful eyes and the most perfect white teeth I had ever seen. But despite her cheerleader good looks, she was a shy bookworm like I was, and I knew she appreciated my nerdiness which had no discernible value in my own home. She also had great taste in music, and Richie would often sneak into her room to snatch records for our dance routines.

After dinner, I helped Richie and Monica with the dishes, and Richie's parents and Grandma Rose sat in the living room watching the news.

Monica immediately started a conversation with me about books.

"What are you reading, Maggie?" Monica asked me as she handed me a plate to dry.

"*A Wizard of Earthsea*," hoping it didn't sound like too babyish a book to be reading at 12.

"Oh my God, I loved that book. Fantasy books are my favorites!" she exclaimed and smiled that same bright smile her brothers had.

"I just finished *Love Story*. So sad, but so amazing," she shared with me.

"Like the movie?" I asked.

"Yes, but the book is so much better," she sighed.

It was so nice to talk about books with someone who loved them as much as I did. Richie said Monica had straight A's and would probably get a scholarship to a great college. She was an excellent role model. Maybe I would tell my mother that.

"Monica, we are all going to Orchard Beach tomorrow for a picnic. Charlie, Gina, Richie, and me. Please come with us. Oh, and Patty might come, if she's not too busy," I rolled my eyes at my sister's claim of a packed social schedule.

"Hey, sounds like a party! I'll be there," Monica replied with a warm smile.

Monica and I had so much fun talking as we scrubbed and dried the dishes, it didn't even seem like a chore. But I knew I had to get home.

"Thank you so much for dinner. It was incredible," I gushed at Richie's parents in the living room before I left.

"You're welcome anytime, Maggie," his mom smiled at me warmly and I knew she meant it. Grandma Rose hugged me on my way out the door.

I got on my bike, feeling 10 pounds heavier from tacos, wondering how I was going to eat another dinner because I certainly couldn't tell my mother I ate with Richie's family without even asking her. But I knew if I had asked, she would've said no, especially after the lecture on the sofa today.

"See ya, Maggie!" Richie waved from the sidewalk as I pedaled away, and when I looked back before I turned the corner, he was still waving, smiling as big as anything.

When I got home, dinner was on the table, but no one seemed to be talking. My sister was still out, and my parents were subdued. I presumed I missed the nightly fight and was just there for the chilly aftermath.

My mother had made goulash, and again it was full of chunky onions and peppers. I stared it down. Not only was I full, but the dinner looked so unappetizing. I was starting to fish out the onions and peppers when I felt her hand on mine.

"Eat your dinner the way I prepared it please," she said sternly. I looked to my father for help, but he clearly had no desire to start or restart an argument with my mother.

"Your mother works hard to make us dinner. Don't complain," he said curtly and took a sip of his Manhattan.

I did my best to gag some down. And a thought occurred to me.

"Could we have tacos for dinner sometime?" I asked sunnily.

"Tacos? We're not Mexican," my mother snipped at me and eyed me suspiciously.

"But we eat spaghetti, and we're not Italian," I replied.

"I don't take dinner orders. This isn't a restaurant," my mother replied sharply, and I knew the conversation was over.

After dinner, I went outside to escape the stifling silence of the house. I walked down the street to where a bunch of younger kids were playing

Kick the Can. I could've joined in, but I didn't feel like it. I just sat on the curb and watched as someone kicked a coffee can down the street, and the rest of them scurried.

I was thinking about the picnic tomorrow and ways I could seem more mature to Charlie. Should I talk about books? Politics? I knew a little bit about the Presidential election from listening to my father pontificate nightly on the subject. I knew I was far too young for Charlie to date now, but I wanted to be sure he knew that I was well on my way to growing up.

I noticed a black car at the end of the street, with a crowd of kids near the driver's side window, so I walked down out of curiosity. A bunch of boys were standing around, looking at Topp's baseball cards. In the car was Father Anthony, and he was joking with them about players and teams. I guess he was handing out the cards to the kids, maybe part of his attempts at youth ministry.

It started to get dark, and the kids playing Kick the Can had gone home, so I walked back to my house. Father Anthony drove by me, but I could see his taillights brake in the distance to hand out a card to another boy.

Everything's Perfect but Me
Tuesday, June 27, 1972

The next morning, I bounded out of bed, excited for our beach picnic. I wanted to look good, but the prospect of wearing my bathing suit made that all but impossible. I dug the gross yellow suit out of the laundry room and desperately tried to find ways to camouflage my body. But as I put on t-shirt after t-shirt, I only felt more dejected with each look in the mirror. The only t-shirt that actually hid my chubbiness had a unicorn on it; what better way to declare how odd I was. I discarded all the clothes on my bed.

Patty knocked on my door and came into my room.

"What's all this? Finally giving away all the hideous clothes?" she cackled at the pile of lame t-shirts on my bed.

"All of my clothes are ugly," I sighed and plopped down on the bed disheartened.

"What took you so long to realize that? You let Mom choose all these shirts," she rifled through my t-shirts and rolled her eyes.

It was true. Since I had to wear a uniform to Catholic school, I had gotten into the habit of wearing whatever my mother bought me. I didn't have it in me to fight with her about my clothes the way Patty did.

"Why this sudden revelation about your horrid wardrobe today?" she asked and sat on my bed with a bounce. As usual, she looked great: Beatles t-shirt, perfect makeup, and scandalously short shorts.

63

"Gina invited me to have a picnic at Orchard Beach with Richie," I explained.

"And is Charlie going to be there?" she asked with a grin. I nodded.

"Put your bathing suit on and I'll take care of the rest," she ordered. I did as she instructed then followed her into her room.

Patty sat me down in her desk chair, although it was really more of a salon chair to her. Patty's lighted makeup mirror, eyeshadows, and lipsticks took up far more space than any school books ever would. My sister's priorities had never been spectacularly academic. I was the family nerd.

I hesitated a little. The last time my sister had offered her cosmetology assistance had been a disaster. The previous September, she had advised me on the night before the first day of sixth grade that I would look far better with bangs. Before I could even consent, she was holding my hair under the sink in our tiny bathroom.

With my hair wet, she cut bangs with scissors she swiped from our mother's sewing kit. I watched her eyes scrunch in concentration and felt a wave of anxiety as I remembered how many of my dolls had suffered unfortunate and permanent haircuts at Patty's hand.

When she finished, my bangs looked okay wet. But as soon as they dried, they curled up into my forehead, and the effect was that of a poorly-groomed poodle. So, I started sixth grade with ratty balls at the back and front of my head.

Today, there were no scissors involved, so I figured it was safe to let her try to improve me, and I was desperate. I was useless on my own.

Patty chose an outfit for me from her clothes: a hot pink t-shirt, a bangly necklace, and a denim mini skirt. I was amazed how easily she created a look. The waistline of the skirt was too tight, but it had elastic, so I could get by. Looking good was worth a stomachache.

Patty then put a little blush on my cheeks and some purple eyeshadow on my lids, and she managed to wrangle my hair into something resembling a braid. She wasn't gentle on my scalp, and I yelped a couple of times, but I felt transformed as I looked at myself in her mirror. Maybe there was hope for me after all.

"What about when I have to swim?" I asked, looking down at my Winnie-the-Pooh stomach.

"Just keep a towel around your waist when you're not in the water. That's what Sandy does," Patty recommended. Sandy was Patty's chubby friend, so I grimaced a bit at her honesty, but appreciated the tip.

"Oh, Gina said, you're invited," I added as an afterthought, assuming my sister had much cooler plans for her day.

"Monica is coming too," I shared, thinking that might increase her interest.

"Oh, that's nice. Well then, I guess I will go," she grinned at me. Her enthusiasm surprised me, and I wondered if Patty hoped her Deadhead boyfriend-to-be would be at the beach.

Our mother was out grocery shopping when we left, so Patty left a note on the fridge: "Picnic at beach with Gina. Be home later. P and M."

Orchard Beach was on the shores of Orchard Pond, a tiny little body of water near the edge of our town. It didn't have sand as much as it had dirt, but in the summer, it was a fun place to cool off and hang out. A few of the wealthier residents of town had camps on the pond, but most people just swam and sunned on the public beach.

The bike ride to the dinky beach was a longer journey than my usual treks, and I had a hard time keeping up with Patty's long, lean legs, steadily pedaling ahead of me. I was pretty winded by the time we arrived, but I did my best to smooth my hair and look relaxed.

Patty brought brownies she'd made yesterday. I wish I had been thoughtful. It hadn't even occurred to me to contribute to the picnic. I needed so much work to be socially acceptable; it exhausted me when I thought about it.

The little beach was pretty crowded, but it didn't take long to find our crew—Gina, Charlie, Richie, and Monica were all sitting on a big floral blanket near a towering pine tree. I waved as we walked up, suddenly self-conscious about my makeup and my outfit. Usually, I strove for invisibility, and I instantly regretted my attempt to look pretty.

"Hello, my favorite girls," Gina stood up and hugged us both tight. Gina was the one person for whom Patty dropped her cool act. She had that effect on people.

"Maggie, you look beautiful," Gina complimented me, standing back to take in my new look. I felt my cheeks burning up as Charlie looked at me too.

"Very hip look, Maggie," Charlie commented with a smile, and I suddenly realized he must have known I was in love with him. I was mortified. I plopped down on the blanket quickly and tried to change the subject.

"What's for lunch?" I asked and instantly regretted it. I sounded like an ungrateful brat, and the last thing I needed to do was draw attention to my chubbiness by asking for food.

"Lots of good stuff," Gina smiled at me and opened her picnic basket. She had packed tuna and PBJ sandwiches, potato chips, Cheese Jax, fresh strawberries, and a couple of thermoses of Kool-Aid with paper cups. Patty handed her the Tupperware container of brownies.

"From Maggie and me," she said with a smile, and I was grateful for my sister's sudden moment of kindness.

"Let's cool off first," Charlie suggested, and whipped off his t-shirt. I tried not to stare at Charlie in just his swim trunks. But his muscles were perfect, and I just about died right there.

Gina took off her tank top but left on her jean shorts with an orange bikini top. Patty shimmied out of her shorts and t-shirt, looking rail thin in her very small hot pink bikini. I was sure Patty had bought it with her own money, and our mother had never seen it. She would have flipped out. Monica had a pretty blue one-piece suit, and I thought how like her it was to wear a modest bathing suit. Her hair was in a taut, precise braid, and she wore no makeup, but she was still one of the prettiest girls I had ever seen. I was always the ugly duckling at every event.

Richie pulled off his t-shirt and sneakers and ran for the water, with Gina and Charlie following him.

With great pain, I pulled off my skirt and t-shirt, to reveal the yellow swimsuit, and following Patty's advice, immediately cloaked my lower half in a towel.

"Maggie, you look fine," Patty offered with a forced smile. Her pity actually made me feel worse.

"Ugh, I hate myself. I'm fat and gross," I mumbled, and Monica looked shocked and pained.

"Maggie, don't say that ever. You're beautiful and amazing!" she responded and gave me a hug.

"Well, that's not exactly the motto we hear at home," Patty laughed, employing her usual sarcasm to lighten the moment.

"What do you mean, Patty?" Monica asked, genuine concern on her face.

Patty and I exchanged awkward glances realizing that not every family inspired self-loathing. We were at a loss to explain it. Besides, Patty hated anyone feeling sorry for her. I felt her pride rise up like an iron fence.

"Nothing, just joking around," Patty said. "Come on, it's too hot to stand around on this dirt sand," she laughed and pulled both of us towards the water.

Patty and Monica dove into the water, but I stayed close to shore, keeping my towel around me as I stuck my feet in the mushy brown dirt. I watched as Charlie splashed Gina and tossed her around in the water. They looked perfect together. Her laugh was so happy and genuine, it almost made me forgive her for looking so beautiful with Charlie.

I wondered if there was any romance between them now that Ray was gone. Charlie certainly looked at her the way I wished he would look at me. And who wouldn't love Gina?

I stood on the shore and just watched other people having fun. Richie kept calling me to go in the water with him, but I just waved him off. I was far too self-conscious for the beach. I knew he didn't understand, but I just couldn't take off the towel and be seen in just my bathing suit. I promised myself to never eat another Twinkie.

Finally, everyone had enough of the water, and we all landed back on the blanket for lunch. I put my skirt and shirt back on over my dry bathing suit, trying to regain some semblance of dignity. I was relieved no one asked why I hadn't really gone swimming.

Charlie had brought a radio, and Chicago's "Saturday in the Park" blared around us. Everyone grabbed a sandwich and a drink, and Gina opened the bags of chips. We all munched away and watched the other swimmers. Two boys were shooting each other with water guns and laughing uproariously. An older couple was wading in the water, hand in hand, and it occurred to me that my parents would never do that, no matter how old they got.

Patty was grilling Monica for information about the public high school. Patty and Monica had always been friendly, but their paths rarely crossed socially because they attended different schools. However, if Patty got her way, she would be at Milford Public with Monica next year, and they would only be one year apart. I wondered if they would be friends, as different as they were.

"Hey Monica, don't those girls go to your school? Do you know them?" Patty asked, pointing at a blanket. Her social sense was always homing in on a more exciting conversation elsewhere.

"Yeah, I'll introduce you if you want," Monica replied politely, and Patty shot up at the opportunity, brushing the sand off her suit and smoothing her hair.

They walked over to a group of girls on a blue blanket. Soon, they were chatting away. Every so often, Patty would throw her head back in a laugh, but I couldn't tell if she was genuinely having fun. She had perfected the art of being a girl: she was an expert at hiding her feelings.

Charlie and Gina were quiet, so I saw a chance to initiate an intelligent conversation with Charlie.

"I think psychology is a very fascinating subject. I might study it in college myself. How was your first class? Did you learn anything unusual?" I asked Charlie and Gina, trying to sound as mature as possible.

Charlie and Gina exchanged quizzical looks at my question, and Richie rolled his eyes and flopped backwards on the blanket, hands on his face, unwilling to watch me gawk at his brother.

"So far, so good," Charlie answered politely. "I'm fairly sure I'll be able to diagnose Richie with a few disorders within a couple of weeks," he teased his brother, and Richie kicked him in the back, hard enough to make a point, but not to do any damage.

"So, what are the big summer plans, guys?" Charlie asked, reclining on his back on the blanket, propped up by his elbows. He was truly a bronze god. I would've been content to just stare at him all day.

Richie popped back up and started eating strawberries, one after the other, so he didn't answer right away. He was a fruit fiend.

"Well, there's the Summer Olympics to watch, and the eclipse, and, of course, the election..." I tried to sound serious and smart.

"Wow, you are interested in the election! Very cool, Maggie," Charlie said with surprise.

"Well, all I have to say is that Nixon better lose," Gina sneered. "He's a war-monger."

"Definitely," I asserted and hoped no one would ask any questions about the candidates. I knew my dad didn't like Nixon and was planning on voting for McGovern. My mother, however, said McGovern was "entirely too liberal for my liking." My mother's disapproval told me he was my candidate.

I was out of conversation already and started pulling out blades of grass. I hated my awkwardness. Richie came to my rescue. He stood up and made a superhero stance, strawberry juice dripping down his face.

"Maggie and I are practicing our dances, so any dance contests this school year, we will slay the competition," he proclaimed, and we all laughed.

After we finished eating, Charlie pulled a soccer ball out of his bag and dragged Richie up to play with him. Richie and Charlie kicked the ball around for a while, and Gina and I watched. Richie was good, as he was at any sport. And I knew his dad would love for him to join the soccer team. I watched Charlie and admired how he controlled the soccer ball, his easy laugh, and his smile. I didn't realize I was smiling as I watched him.

"Oh boy, Maggie, you have it bad," Gina teased me, and again my red cheeks betrayed me.

"I know," I said quietly.

"Well, you couldn't have chosen a better person for a crush. Charlie is about the nicest guy who ever lived," she commented. Gina laid back on the blanket and shut her eyes to soak up the sun. She looked like a Coppertone model.

"So, do you like him, Gina?" I asked the question that had tormented me as I watched them splash in the water.

"Oh, Maggie, no way," she protested. "He's too nice for me. Plus, he's like my brother. I've known him forever. I have issues. I have this thing for bad boys. Lord, help me," she laughed and reached for the suntan lotion. She started to apply it to her legs.

"I can never get my legs to tan," she remarked casually, even though her skin looked perfect to me, way tanner than my Irish skin would ever be.

For the first time, I felt envy and even a bit of resentment towards Gina. What would it be like to be so pretty? What if she secretly did like Charlie, or he liked her? Gina sensed me looking at her and stared at me.

"Maggie, hand on my heart, there is nothing between Charlie and me. We are family. No romance at all," she swore solemnly. It was like she could read my mind.

"Okay, Gina," I replied awkwardly, ashamed of my jealousy. I should want Gina to have Charlie. He was never going to look at me anyway.

The radio was playing Rod Stewart's "You Wear it Well." I lay down on my stomach and shut my eyes. The sun was hot, but it felt good. There was a breeze, and the world seemed very peaceful.

"Beautiful day, Maggie. I wish everyday could be this perfect," Gina sighed, sounding suddenly sad.

"Are you upset about Ray, Gina?" I asked, wondering how it felt to lose someone you had for two years. I still didn't know what happened. Relationships were such a mystery to me.

"That's a tough question. I feel sad I hurt him," she answered, sitting up and crossing her legs, suddenly restless. I sat up next to her.

"Did you love him?" I asked cautiously, worried it was way too personal a question. But Gina seemed unfazed.

"I thought I loved Ray, but I don't know. Love is confusing," she told me with a somber smile.

"I thought you just knew when you loved someone." I offered, wondering if my parents loved each other at all. I was sure I loved Charlie.

"If you find the right person, I guess maybe you do," she answered a bit sadly.

"Ray wasn't the right person?" I asked.

"No, I mean Ray is a sweet guy in lots of ways. But we just didn't connect in lots of other ways. He is a very basic dude. Car, beer, food, me," she laughed. Gina absentmindedly rubbed the necklace with her name.

"But he loves you?" I countered.

"He does. And I tried, but it just wasn't going to work," she said and looked at the water, her face suddenly very troubled. Then she looked at me again.

"The thing is sometimes love isn't enough. I want more, you know?" she explained, and I wondered what she meant.

"Like what?" I was curious what more she could want than a cute guy who loved her.

"Someone to talk to about the future, you know. Someone who thinks about life beyond this town," she sighed, seeming frustrated. Her eyes scanned the beach, as if she was watching for someone.

"You will find that guy," I promised her, nodding.

"Sometimes, it's more complicated than that," she sighed.

"What do you mean, Gina?" I probed, confused.

Gina paused for a minute, and then seemed to shake off a thought and smiled at me.

"Nothing. Love is a great thing and you will find love too, Maggie May, in time. You should just enjoy being 12 and on the brink of everything. Sometimes I wish I was 12 again," she tried to reassure me, but I felt frustrated that she was ignoring all the bad parts of being me.

"But you weren't like me at 12. You were pretty and popular," I reminded her.

"Everybody has their stuff, Maggie, even if it all looks great from the outside," she reminded me. I knew Gina had a tough life in some ways, with no dad and her mom always struggling with money, but I doubted the girls who were mean to me at school had it rough.

"I don't know. I just can't wait to be older. I'm tired of being a kid. Everyone thinks being a kid is so great, but it's not," I said bitterly.

"What's bugging you, Maggie?" Gina asked with concern. I didn't know where to start. There was far too much to ever explain on a sunny day at the beach.

"I'm just tired of everyone telling me what's wrong with me," I tried to sum up my feelings.

"Do you mean your mom?" Gina asked.

"Yeah, but not just her. Other kids. I just want to grow up and be able to get away from all of them," I huffed and felt tears unexpectedly forming in my eyes. I willed them to stop. I hated how easily I cried.

"Listen, Maggie. You know I respect your mom. But she's not easy to please. It's not you. Nothing quite lives up to her expectations from what I can tell," Gina tried to console me.

72

"But especially me. And I can't talk to her about anything," I confessed.

"Well, you can always talk to me," she said with a gentle smile.

"Thanks, Gina. I hope I am just like you when I grow up," I told her, grateful I had her as a role model. I certainly didn't want to be like my mother.

"No, Maggie, you are a way better person than I am," she said firmly. I had no idea why she said that. I would be lucky to be half as amazing as Gina.

"You're the best person I know. You're perfect," I complimented her. Gina got a strange look on her face.

"I am so far from perfect, Maggie. No one is perfect, and you can't expect people to be. Please don't idolize me. I'm a mess," she said, sounding frustrated.

"No, you're not. You're everything I want to be," I argued.

"Maggie, trust me. Don't idolize anyone, especially me," she repeated, and I could hear something very sad in her voice. It scared me.

"Okay," I promised, worried I had upset her.

Gina took a deep breath, paused, and spoke again, "Listen, you don't need to be like anyone, but yourself. You are an amazing person, and you will just get more amazing as you grow up. Just give yourself time," she advised me.

Just then, our favorite song "Close to You" by the Carpenters came on the radio. We looked at each other and grinned. Then we sang it together loudly and probably very off-key. It described how I felt about Charlie perfectly: "Why do stars fall down from the sky, every time you walk by?" When we finished, we laughed.

"See, Maggie, love makes you c-r-a-z-y crazy!" she hollered and laughed again. And just like that, whatever had been bothering her evaporated.

She stood up suddenly, and ran to join the soccer game, so I followed.

Gina was pretty athletic, but I was sorely lacking soccer skills. Charlie insisted I try anyway, and even gave me a few pointers which made the experience worth it.

Eventually, the four of us reconvened on the blanket for some more Kool-Aid. It seemed we had lost Patty and Monica to the blanket of high school girls for the rest of the afternoon. My sister sure knew how to work a crowd.

Richie was entertaining us with stories about the guys at his dad's garage, and his impersonation of Big Richie when he was mad.

"I was in my room, not tired, so I was practicing a dance. My dad wanted me to sleep. He comes in all serious, like, 'Now listen, son, not another peep! You hear me?'" he imitated his father's deep voice.

"After he left the room, I said 'Peep,' and he comes flying through the door. 'Did I hear a peep?' he says. And I said, 'maybe Peep, I mean Pop,'" Richie was roaring at his story, holding his stomach laughing.

"Did you get in trouble?" I asked. I couldn't imagine teasing either of my parents that way.

"Naw, I could tell he wanted to laugh too. No trouble, but I did have to go to bed," he explained, and I realized he didn't fear his parents at all.

The rest of the gang took another swim to cool off, but I was done in from all my emotions, the heat, and how I felt in my stupid yellow bathing suit. I sat on the blanket and watched Richie jumping in the water. Patty was telling a story to the hive of girls, and they were laughing uproariously. Monica laughed along.

Gina and Charlie were wading in the water. They appeared to be having a serious conversation, and after something he said, she splashed some water in his direction, turned abruptly and walked back to the blanket. She laid down without saying a word and shut her eyes. I was afraid to say the wrong thing, so I just kept quiet.

By 4 pm, we were all tired from the sun and heat. Gina and Monica folded up her blanket and put the leftover food in the picnic basket. We said our goodbyes, and Gina hugged Patty and me. Charlie gave me a wink and little hug with his goodbye, which would keep me happy for days.

Gina, Charlie, Monica, and Richie piled into Charlie's car and beeped as they drove past us. As Patty and I rode our bikes home in the late afternoon sun, I felt happy and sad. I loved being with everyone, but I was just never comfortable in my own skin, and I wondered if I ever would be.

As I lay in bed that night, I thought about my conversation with Gina. Even on the sunniest days, there was always something stirring beneath the surface. Gina had secrets, but I shouldn't be surprised. I had my own secrets. Outside, I could hear crickets and a distant owl making their eerie night sounds. I hugged my dolls and realized everyone, even Gina, was a mystery to me.

No Matter What

Wednesday, June 28, 1972

The next day, Richie decided our roller-skating had improved enough to make the bold move of skating at Fancy's Roller Rink, our small town's answer to a disco, nightclub, and roller rink all in one. At night, it was adults only, and they served alcoholic drinks, although I couldn't imagine how people roller skated while drunk. It was hard enough sober. But during the day, they had skating times for kids.

My mother had commented before that Fancy's was a sleazy establishment, and I am fairly sure had I asked, she would've told me I couldn't go. So, I didn't ask. I knew from religion class that was called a sin of omission, but I figured in the hierarchy of sins, that was better than an outright lie.

I rode my bike to Richie's and then together we sped towards Fancy's in our small downtown area. My roller skates wouldn't fit in my bike basket, so I slung them over the seat of my bike; they were banging against me with every pedal. I would be bruised before we ever started skating.

We arrived at Fancy's and locked up our bikes at the stand in front. Fancy's had originally been a bowling alley, and from the outside, it still looked like one. But instead of the giant plaster bowling pin that had once stood by the door, there was now a huge plaster roller skate covered in pink glitter. We walked out of the sunshine into the strobe lights and loud music of Fancy's.

Once inside, it could have been day or night, summer or winter. The orange carpet was torn from years of roller skates trekking across it, but the rink was fantastic—shiny wooden planks polished for action. Lime-green plastic benches were placed by the various entrances onto the rink.

Richie and I sat down on one and put our skates on. I felt butterflies in my stomach. I could skate now but stopping required falling or hitting a wall. Richie, on the other hand, was practically a pro, and the skating rink was the closest thing to a dancing venue that we had in town.

With trepidation, I entered the rink, Richie racing ahead of me excitedly. It wasn't terribly crowded, but there were enough teenagers whizzing around that I had to be careful not to smack into them or have them collide with me as I careened haphazardly around the rink.

The sound system was blasting Stevie Wonder's "For Once in My Life," and Richie, clad in blue shorts, red tank top, and gym socks, was a dancing, skating machine. I watched him dance while he skated, his little afro blowing in the skating breeze and his happiest smile. At times, he closed his eyes, feeling the music. I trailed behind him just trying to stay upright. I had worn jeans to protect me from the inevitable falls, but they were proving less than comfortable in the heat of the rink.

Watching Richie skate, I knew he would be a choreographer one day. Movement was natural to him, and he looked blissful when the music was playing, and he was moving. As Richie flowed across the rink, I wiped out numerous times. But every time, he was there in a flash to pull me up and get me going again.

After about an hour of skating, I was sore and sweaty, and I exited the rink for a break. I watched Richie whirl and boogie to "Let's Stay Together" by Al Green. When the song finished, he looked for me and finally spied me sitting on the bench. He popped off the rink and sat down next to me.

"You okay?" he asked, having witnessed several spectacular falls.

"Yeah, more embarrassed than anything," I replied with a sigh.

"Mags, don't be embarrassed. You did great. And you got back up every time," he encouraged me.

"Thanks, but I still can't stop without hitting a wall," I said with a laugh.

"All you need is a root beer," he reassured me with a grin.

"Okay," I agreed, and we unlaced our skates and walked over to the snack bar in our socks. I was relieved I didn't see anyone from school here. It must have been a Milford Public hangout. I'm sure the nuns had warned everyone at Saint Christopher's about the dangers of roller rinks and the speedy sins committed on skates.

As we got in the long line for sodas, I saw a look cross Richie's face. I traced his glance to a group of boys standing around a table near the snack bar. They looked to be around my age. As we got closer to the counter, one of them shouted at us. I knew then the look on Richie's face was fear.

"Hey Richie, we saw you out there!" a boy chided him in a singsong voice. The boy was homely with bad skin and red hair, and his facial expression revealed malice. Richie just ignored him.

"Who are those guys, Richie?" I asked with concern.

"Nobody," he answered stoically.

Next to the redhead was a lanky boy with ghostly-white skin and black hair. He called out next.

"Hey Fairy Boy, we saw you prancing around the rink. You put on a real show," he laughed derisively at Richie, and the other boys followed suit.

I suddenly became aware of what Richie's school life was like, and my heart broke. But Richie just stood there looking straight ahead.

"Hey Richie, I'm talking to you. Turn around, you faggot!" the red-headed, acne-faced boy shouted angrily.

Richie took my hand and we walked away quickly, laughter spraying behind us. Wordlessly, we put our sneakers back on, took our skates, and walked into the blinding sunshine to our bikes.

"Richie, are you okay? Who were those guys?" I asked softly as we mounted our bikes.

"Like I said, they're nobody who matters," he answered through gritted teeth.

"Are they always like that at school?" I asked tentatively.

"Sometimes. I usually avoid them, ignore them," he answered flatly. I nodded. I understood all too well.

"Let's go to Watson's for root beer," he suggested, and we took off on our bikes. I followed Richie on his bike, and I felt so angry that Richie's happy skating day had been ruined by the ugliness of those boys.

We arrived at Watson's and leaned our bikes against the side of the building.

Watson's Market was a regular stop of ours, along with Rollins Drugstore, right next door. Both were across the street from East Milford High School, so they did steady business. Usually, we would go to Rollins first to dig through the record bins, looking for our favorite songs. Then head to Watson's to buy penny candy, sodas, and comic books. I always got Atomic Fire Balls because I liked seeing how long I could stand the cinnamon burning my mouth before I had to crunch it. But Richie liked Swedish Fish, and without fail, he would shove a bunch in his mouth at once all in one cheek and do his Popeye imitation and dance.

Since we were both parched from skating, we skipped the drugstore and went directly into Watson's. The five-dollar bill from Gina and one from my grandma were burning a hole in my pocket, so I insisted on buying our food and comics. We bought more than our usual haul, adding Mallow Cups and Peanut Butter Cups to our order. I bought an *Archie's* comic for myself, and the latest *Richie Rich* for Richie, his namesake and hero. Richie insisted someday he would live in luxury like Richie Rich.

With our candy and comics in hand, we stood outside and sipped our root beers, pressing the cold glass to our foreheads to cool us down. As we mounted our bikes, we saw Uncle Jimmy standing by the side door of the high school gym, smoking a cigarette. He looked sweaty and his stomach was pudging out under his t-shirt. He was leaning on an industrial broom. I waved at him, but he didn't see me because he was watching the girls' field hockey team practice.

"Isn't that your uncle?" Richie said and pointed at Uncle Jimmy.

"Yeah, that's him," I answered, embarrassed.

"Want to go over and say hi?" he offered because in his family that would have been the normal thing to do. But my family wasn't normal, and I didn't particularly like Uncle Jimmy.

"Nah, he's busy," I explained, although the only thing he was busy doing was staring at teenage girls. I felt a sudden shiver looking at him.

We got on our bikes and headed to the front lawn of the high school to eat our candy and read our comics. We let our bikes fall on the grass and sat against the trunk of an old oak tree. But neither of us felt much like eating or reading. We watched some teenagers playing Frisbee, both of us lost in thought.

"Maggie, what are you thinking?" Richie asked me nervously.

"I just don't get people," I answered vaguely. We both sat quiet for a minute.

"I know what you mean," he sighed. "I'm sorry that happened at Fancy's and we had to leave. I was so embarrassed," he confessed, shutting his eyes and shaking his head.

"You shouldn't be embarrassed. Those boys were jerks. Stuff like that happens to me too. You know that," I reminded him.

"But what they said about me," he said softly.

"They don't know you," I reassured him, and he looked away.

"What if they're right?" he whispered.

I thought for a minute, not knowing what to say. I had heard the ugly word "faggot" before and I knew what it meant. Patty had once gone on a choral trip to sing at a church in Greenwich Village in New York City, and before the concert, the choir ate at a pizza place in the Village. When Patty got home, she told me there were lots of men there who were gay. They held hands and kissed each other. The nuns had a fit.

I didn't really understand because I always had crushes on boys. In second grade, I was obsessed with Michael Fitzpatrick, the cute blond-haired boy who sat next to me in class. One day, he asked to borrow my treasured felt-tip flair markers. I used the brightly colored markers to draw illustrations for my writing. But I willingly gave them up to Michael with a smile. The next day, my teacher Sister Claire announced that Michael Fitzpatrick had moved, taking my markers with him it seemed. Thus was my introduction to matters of the heart. Shortly thereafter I set my sights solely on Charlie. Although he was older, he was far sweeter than any of the boys in my class, and no one in town was as handsome as Charlie.

But as far as I knew, Richie had never had a crush on a girl, never expressed an interest in anyone. And I knew our friendship would always stay just that. We were like siblings, not a hint of romance in the air. I didn't know if that made him gay.

But I did know that none of it mattered. I knew Richie better than I knew anyone on earth, and everything about him was good and sweet and pure. Whatever or whoever he was, I loved him.

"It doesn't matter to me. You're my best friend," I answered. "You'll always be my best friend. That will never change, no matter what," I promised.

Richie was quiet, but I looked at him and he had tears on his face.

"No matter what?" he whispered nervously.

"I swear, Richie. Nothing will ever change us," I promised him.

"I'm closer to you than my family, Mags," he said softly.

"Me too, with you," I answered back. "*My* family doesn't get me at all," I sighed.

Richie seemed to ponder something for a minute as he pulled at a blade of grass.

"Maggie, can I ask you something?" he said quietly.

"Sure," I responded, nervously, unsure what he might ask.

"Why *is* your mom so hard on you?" he said gently.

First, I shrugged, cause damned if I knew. But then I thought about it.

"I'm just nothing like her. She doesn't like me or understand me. She was this prom queen, and I'm just me," I explained. He nodded in sympathy. I realized at that moment that he truly was the closest family I had, and I suddenly wanted him to know my secrets.

"And I guess I'm pretty mad at her. Because there's this bad stuff about my grandfather I never told anyone, and I know she'd never believe me even if I told her...." I trailed off. I couldn't finish. My voice was hoarse with shame.

Richie's eyes widened, and I felt my stomach flop in panic.

"What kind of bad stuff?" he asked softly.

I squeezed my eyes tight against the memory. "Things he did to me...I can't," I whispered. But I didn't need to say another word. He got it. He just knew. For a moment, I was terrified. I expected him to run away, but he took my hand and held it tight.

"Sorry, Maggie," he said gently. I felt myself start to cry, and we just sat there holding hands for a while.

Finally, Richie spoke, "You okay?" he asked hesitantly.

I took a deep breath. "I'm fine," I said. And I was. Better than fine, I was relieved. For the first time, I had spoken about what happened in that bathroom, even if I didn't say much. And Richie hadn't run away. He still loved me, and he always would.

We sat for a while, under the tree, thinking, comforted by just being together. Then suddenly, Richie smiled.

"You know, Maggie, this candy isn't going to eat itself," he said, and he shoved an entire Peanut Butter Cup in his mouth, grinning. I laughed and did the same. Pretty soon, we were both laughing at nothing and everything at once.

"Oh, man, Maggie, when you wiped out on the rink that one time, I thought for sure there would be blood," Richie teased me and fell over laughing.

"Tell me about it. I have bruises already," I laughed back at him.

"Maybe you should stick to dancing for a while, leave the wheels at home," he advised grinning.

"Or maybe I should just work on walking," I joked back, and he laughed harder. Lord knows, I tripped over my own feet all too often.

We finished most of our candy but were too full for the Swedish fish and FireBalls, so we packed up our remaining treats, mounted our bikes, and headed for home.

As we pedaled in the late afternoon light, I felt so happy. No matter what else happened in life, I had one true friend.

Flips and Twists

Thursday, June 29, 1972

Richie and I would usually only see each other during the day because our parents wouldn't let us walk or bike home at night from each other's houses. They didn't trust us to get home before dark; we had a tendency to lose track of time.

Evening activities for children were pretty much out of the question anyway. Generally, my parents like to wrap the day up with their kids as quickly as possible. Up until about fourth grade, my bedtime was so ridiculously early, I would be sent to bed in the summer when it was still light out, and I could clearly hear the neighborhood kids playing kickball through my bedroom window.

But Richie and I were determined to find a way to get him to my house on Thursday night because the Summer Olympics were in full swing, and gymnastics was on Thursday and Friday nights. Both Richie and I were obsessed with Russian gymnast Olga Korbut's flips and splits, especially on the balance beam.

My father even built us a small balance beam out of lumber left over from our back deck. The balance beam was about six inches off the ground, but it was enough for Richie and me to walk, preen, and invent dramatic dismounts, pretending we were Olympic gymnasts.

Richie and I formulated a plan. Friday night was out because both his parents would be home, but on Thursday nights his mom worked at the hospital and his grandma attended a Bible study at a neighbor's house. That left just his dad who always fell asleep on the couch, so Richie could easily escape. Then he could sneak home after the Olympics, and his parents would never even know he had been out.

On Thursday, I made sure to be particularly good all day, and after dinner, I pitched my request. I knew Richie was waiting for my call to confirm our plans.

My parents were sitting in their wingback chairs in the front living room, cocktails aloft, reading the evening paper. Both seemed in good moods. We'd had pizza for dinner, a rare summertime weekday treat, so Mom was relaxed with no dishes to clean, and for once they weren't fighting, despite the tinkling glasses of Scotch and Manhattan.

"Hey Mom and Dad, do you think Richie could come over tonight and watch the Olympics with me? Gymnastics is on. Olga Korbut," I tried to sound as sweet as possible.

They both looked at me over their newspapers, my mother with a sour expression, my dad's face unreadable.

"Margaret Grace, you know that Richie cannot go home in the dark by himself," she answered curtly, and raised her paper back up, considering the matter settled. It annoyed me that she was voicing concern for Richie when she really just didn't want him to come over.

"Can his parents drive him home?" my dad asked unexpectedly, and my mother put her paper back down looking very annoyed.

"His mom works on Thursdays, and they only have one car right now. But he can ride his bike. It's fine," I explained, feeling my mother's disapproval.

"Hmm," my dad replied and seemed to think for a minute. "I'll run him home in the car after the Olympics," he offered, and I nearly fell over. Our parents were not in the habit of driving us anywhere. The car was for work and adult outings, like the grocery store and bridge nights, not for ferrying the likes of us around.

My mother shot him a death stare. But he put his newspaper back up, and the conversation ended.

I didn't wait for any rebuttal from my mother. As I ran to the phone, I could hear a slight squabble; it sounded like the typical monologue of my mom complaining about me and my lack of friends. I ignored it and dialed. My mother's sense of decorum would not allow her to make me uninvite Richie after I had told him he was invited. As much as she didn't want him in our house, she wouldn't want to seem inhospitable in any way. She had steely internal rules about etiquette, as she was under the illusion that she had some kind of reputation to maintain.

I excitedly told Richie to come over, that my dad would drive him home. He was excited and relieved that he would not have to sneak out. When I came back into the living room, my mother was gone. I looked out the kitchen window and saw her sitting on the back deck, reading a magazine. She was obviously angry, but it was a quiet anger, at least for now.

I went outside to sit on the front steps to wait for Richie to trek the 10-minute ride to my house. As I sat, I pondered what my father would be like if he had married a different woman. Maybe he would be a happy person, willing to drive me anywhere, welcoming my friends over regularly. But I pictured my mother's stricken face, and I immediately felt guilty.

Outside waiting for Richie to arrive, I saw Mr. and Mrs. Johnson taking a walk with their beautiful baby in a stroller. Daisy was now a chubby ten-month-old in a pink bonnet. I waved, and they stopped in front of my house, so I could admire her.

"She's adorable," I played peek-a-boo with Daisy, and she giggled at me. She had the cutest little sandals on her chubby pink feet, and I thought she was perfection.

"Thank you, Maggie. She is certainly a handful," Mrs. Johnson remarked, smiling down at her baby.

Mrs. Johnson certainly didn't look like she'd ever had a baby. She was tiny. On this occasion, she wore a floral dress and floppy hat to walk the baby, and a full face of makeup, too. Around her neck, she wore a silver pendant in the shape of a half-moon. She was glamorous. She worked part-time at a local department store, and from the look of it spent most of her money on expensive clothes.

My mother didn't approve of Mrs. Johnson's job. She was very skeptical of a mother who would choose to work over taking care of her baby. But I knew Gina was as good as any mom, and she was their sitter.

I asked Gina once if she thought mothers should work, and she told me that women's talents absolutely should not be wasted. Gina gave me an article to read by a feminist named Gloria Steinem in *New York Magazine*. I loved how Gloria talked about women's rights. When my mother found the magazine on my bed, she called Gloria Steinem an enemy of the Holy Roman Church and threw the magazine out in disgust. But I decided Gina and Gloria were right; I would work and have a family.

As I tickled her feet, Daisy was giggling at me with four adorable teeth showing.

"She likes you, Maggie. Soon, you'll be old enough to babysit for Daisy," Mrs. Johnson offered with a smile, adjusting Baby Daisy's hat to shield her from the sun.

"But you have Gina," I reminded her.

"Gina's very busy with school, so we will need someone new soon," Mr. Johnson explained, and smiled at me for so long, I felt myself blush. It made sense that they would need a new sitter. Gina would be a full-time student in the fall.

"Okay, sure, let me know," I replied with a smile. I would love to get a glimpse inside the house of this TV perfect couple. I imagined it was decorated with funky beads, lava lamps, and bean bag chairs.

As they strolled away holding hands, I dreamed that one day I would have a cool house and a great marriage. And, of course, that immediately made me think of Charlie. Our baby would be an adorable mini version of him.

Suddenly, Ray's car sped down the street, far too fast considering the Johnsons were walking their baby. He screeched to a stop in front of our house, Led Zeppelin blaring from his speakers.

He rolled his window down and lowered the volume, "Have you seen Gina?" he shouted at me, a cigarette dangling from his mouth. He looked as handsome as ever, but his eyes were hooded and dark, like a wolf.

I just shook my head no. He stared at me for a minute as if trying to ascertain my truthfulness.

"If you see her, tell her I'm looking for her. I need to talk to her," he shot back gruffly. As an afterthought, he added, "Please." Then he turned up Zeppelin and gunned the car, his tires squealing as he took off.

I knew Gina had broken up with Ray, so I was kind of unnerved by his desperation. He always seemed so gruff. But part of me felt sorry for him too.

Gina had once shown me Ray's house when we were taking a long bike ride. The front yard of the house was crowded with all sorts of car parts and other orphaned mechanical items, and the paint on the house was peeling which was ironic given the family profession. Gina said Ray lived with his dad, and that his mom lived in an apartment a few towns over, and Ray seldom saw her. It was a sad-looking house.

I was snapped out of my reverie by Richie running up the block, a huge smile on his face.

"Where's your bike?" I shouted my question down the street to him.

"I ran here," he hollered back, "and look!" He directed me to watch him as he turned awkward cartwheels down the sidewalk until he ended up in front of me.

"Ta-da!" he declared and took a bow.

"When did you learn to do cartwheels?" I asked in amazement.

"Taught myself today," he grinned. As always, his ability to make his body do whatever he commanded amazed me.

We spent the next half hour trying to do cartwheels and handsprings on my front lawn. I was pitiful, but Richie seemed to improve with every attempt. Eventually, it was time to watch the real thing. I felt like I had to prepare Richie for an evening in my house. I sat down on the front steps and Richie sat beside me.

"Richie, do your parents ever fight?" I asked him hesitantly.

"Sure, sometimes, my mom leaves the car outside, and it rains, my dad is like, 'Maria, I just waxed the car!'" Richie replied, doing an impersonation of his dad, laughing at his dad's frustration. He wasn't getting it.

"No, I mean like really fight. Like screaming, yelling, swearing fights," I tried to clarify. Richie looked puzzled.

"Um, not really. Yours do?" he asked gently. Usually, my parents refrained from fighting in front of anyone but family, but lately the fighting had escalated, and I was afraid there could be an explosion while Richie was there. I wasn't sure my mom considered him proper enough company to swallow her anger. As close as Richie and I were, it was too embarrassing to tell him what really went on in my house until I had to.

"Yeah, and it's been bad lately. So, if it happens, we can just come out here, okay?" I asked. Richie took a moment to think, and then nodded.

"Like a fire drill," Richie said with a smile. I laughed.

"Yeah, but trust me, they are way louder than the fire alarm at school," I advised him and rolled my eyes.

Having been duly warned, Richie got up and we went inside. My father was sitting in his chair in the living room, and we settled on the floor in front of the TV.

I scooted into the kitchen to get us cans of root beer, a couple of moon pies, and some pretzels, and we waited for Olga to do her thing. Richie was talking happily as he munched away, crumbs going everywhere, so relaxed. Crumbs in Richie's house were a sign of a happy family enjoying food. But in my house, crumbs were a sign of the apocalypse, so I cleaned them up immediately before they caught my mother's eagle eye.

When Olga finally came on, Richie was so excited by her flipping and twisting, he could hardly sit still. I thought he was going to do a cartwheel right in our living room, shattering my mother's China as he landed.

But as I looked back at my father, he was smiling. My mom passed through on her way to her bedroom. I was sure she'd spend the rest of the evening alone reading and sulking. I saw her glance at our bowl of pretzels, and I was glad I had cleaned up the crumbs.

"Hey, Mrs. Murphy! Thanks for having me over," Richie gave her a big hello and a smile.

My mom smiled back at him, "Our pleasure," she said, and it sounded very nearly sincere. Then she retreated to her bedroom, and I breathed a sigh of relief that there would likely be no fight tonight.

As the night wore on, Richie and I were both lying on our stomachs on the floor watching all the gymnasts amaze us. At around 9:30, my dad announced it was time for Richie to go home. I asked if Richie could look through the telescope first. Like me, Richie loved the stars and dreaming of the endless possibilities in the Milky Way. Dad agreed, and we both followed him into the study.

"Come here, Richie," Dad invited Richie to look through the lens into the night sky, which was full of stars.

"Whoa," Richie said, his voice full of wonder. Dad took the lens back and focused it. Then he guided Richie to look again.

"That's Ursa Major and Ursa Minor," Dad explained.

"Do you believe in aliens?" Richie asked my dad, his eyes alive with curiosity.

"It's certainly possible," Dad admitted. Richie and I took turns looking through the telescope, silently in awe of the mysterious night sky.

"Can we use this for the eclipse?" Richie asked.

"No, you can't look directly at the sky during an eclipse. It can blind you," Dad cautioned.

Richie and I were both excited at the prospect of the August eclipse. The sun disappearing during the day was like something out of a fantasy novel. It seemed magical.

"Okay, kids, time to call it a night," Dad said gently, and we followed him out of the study.

I wanted to ride with Richie as Dad drove him home, but my father asked me to stay with my mother instead. I think he wanted me to make peace before he had to go into their bedroom. It was the least I could do since he had been so nice.

Richie bounced off to my dad's car, talking all the way about how he was going to teach himself to do all the tricks the gymnasts did.

I reluctantly went to my parents' bedroom and knocked on the door.

"Come in," my mother called out.

I stepped into the room, and my mother was sitting in a chair near the window, still reading her magazine. She didn't look up at me when I entered, and I felt the usual fear that was part of talking to her.

"Thanks, Mom, for letting Richie come over tonight. It was really fun," I offered my thanks, and she was silent. She continued to flip the pages of her magazine. She was in her dark burgundy robe, her hair pulled tautly back in a bun. It looked painful.

"I appreciate it," I tried again to convey my gratitude.

"Thank your father. It was his decision," she reminded me coldly and shot me an icy glare. I shut the door, wondering how she always managed to find just the right way to hurt my feelings.

Pressure Drops

Friday, June 30, 1972

The next day was a boring day of Friday chores. I was assigned the dreaded task of cleaning the downstairs bathroom. Must have been my punishment for having Richie over the previous night. Since it was our only full bathroom, it saw a lot of use. Cleaning it involved scrubbing the tub with Clorox and a scratchy sponge. As always, my mother reminded me she would be inspecting my work. I toiled away, thinking how when I was a big, famous writer, I would have a maid.

My parents were having one of their bridge nights on Saturday, and my mother felt a spotless house would be a reflection of her character, and I wondered if her "friends" would really look in our tub when they came over for bridge. I bet she looked in other people's tubs. I imagined my mother pulling back the shower curtain in Mrs. Conway's house to assess her worth as a human being.

When I finished the tub, I hid in my room and read. I knew if I tried to go anywhere my mother would assign me another chore, possibly something worse like polishing silver. There was no escaping the house today.

Later in the day, I played badminton in the backyard with Patty. Dinner was cube steak, one of my least favorite meals, but I hadn't said a word about dinner since the taco suggestion. I smothered the cube steak—

which had the consistency of a rubber-soled sandal—with ketchup and gagged it down. I could see my mother watching me, just daring me to complain, but I knew better. I was still on thin ice from my surgical removal of the peppers and onions from her meatloaf.

After dinner, I headed outside and found some girls from school jumping rope. I ventured over, hoping to kind of sidle in unobtrusively, but one of the mean girls, Katie, spied me first. Katie wore glasses, was chubby like me, and like me didn't live in the rich suburbs. I always wondered how she had made it into the coven, but I supposed relentless groveling eventually pays off.

"Hey, it's Haggy Maggie!" she cackled. "Where's your colored husband?" she laughed, and the other girls giggled in a chorus of ridicule.

"Don't say colored. It's rude. Say Black," I informed her. I couldn't believe how many people refused to use the right word.

"Whatever, okay. Your Black, sissy husband!" she hissed back. The other girls just stared, waiting for me to respond. But as usual, I froze. Instead of responding, I turned around and went home. I could hear the jump rope hitting the pavement, punctuating their laughter as I walked away.

I wanted to watch the Olympics again, but when I went back into the house, my parents were watching some news show on PBS, and I knew better than to push my luck. So instead, I trotted upstairs to the small sanctuary of my room.

Once in my room, I changed into my PJ's and put some 45's on my record player. My sister had gone to the mall and brought me back my new favorites, "Puppy Love" by my beloved Donny Osmond, and "Brandy" by some band called Looking Glass. "Brandy" was about a beautiful girl that all the sailors in a small fishing town loved.

Maybe when I was older, I would change my name to Brandy, and that would somehow magically transform my looks too. I got out my journal to start writing, when I heard the screen door slam and my sister arrive home with her usual dramatic flair.

Then I heard my sister scream. I sighed, thinking another fight was starting, and it was late for that nonsense. Fights that started after dinner almost always meant my dad was drunk and they usually were blow-outs. I tried to ignore the yelling and continued writing in my journal.

I was trying to catalog every day of the summer in anticipation of something interesting happening at some point. I was determined my chronicle of days would lead up to some excitement. Maybe after the eclipse, the sun would never reappear.

It got quiet again downstairs, so I assumed the reprisal of an earlier fight was done. But you never knew when things might explode again. I decided to stay put in my room and read.

Suddenly, my sister burst through my door, tears streaming down her face. She came over and hugged me. It was so out of character, I drew back from her. My family was not usually affectionate this way. I wondered what my mother had said to upset my sister so much.

"Maggie, something awful happened," she choked out. I immediately thought Grandma had died, and I felt guilty that I wasn't able to summon up the proper level of grief.

"Is it Grandma?" I asked hesitantly, trying to sound appropriately sad.

"No. I was hanging out with Sandy down by the school path, and a cop came by," Patty was hiccupping as she talked, trying to contain her tears.

I looked up to see both of my parents standing in my doorway. This was getting weirder by the minute. I felt like I was watching the scene staring down from the ceiling, like a play in which I didn't have an actual part. A ghoulish kind of Nativity Play.

"Okay," I said, watching them all suspiciously, wary of whatever revelation was heading towards me.

"The cop said we should go home because they found a body on Pirates Island," Patty continued slowly now, as my parents watched her.

Pirates Island was a cluster of trees about a half-mile wide and deep, in between the Milford Middle School and High School playing fields.

Athletes often sat at its edges for shade during games, and high school students hid in the thicket of trees, skipping school to smoke pot.

"Like a person's body?" I asked, still finding the entire conversation bizarre.

My father came and sat next to me on the bed, and I scooched in the corner, trying to get away from all of them and whatever awful thing they were about to say.

"Maggie, I want you to take a deep breath. This is really hard to tell you, but I think it's best you hear it now when we are all home with you," my father said slowly, and I could tell he was speaking with great effort.

I felt as if stones were weighing my body down in one place. I thought of Richie, and I prayed that no one would utter his name.

"Honey, it's Gina. She's dead," my father said the sentence that changed everything. I sat stunned for a moment. It was like someone had slammed me in the chest.

"No, you're lying," I said and slapped at my father to get away from me.

"Maggie, I'm so sorry," my mother finally spoke, and at that moment, I hated her.

"Why are you doing this? Who makes up a sick lie like this?" I screamed at my mother.

"Maggie, it's not a lie. I'm so sorry. It's true and it's awful," my father said softly.

"Gina would never go to Pirates Island, so it can't be her. They just have her mixed up with someone else. I'm going to call her," I yelled. I pushed past my family and ran downstairs to the telephone in the kitchen.

I dialed Gina's number, but it was busy. I tried three more times, and it was busy every time.

I looked up and my family was in the kitchen watching me.

"See, she's on the phone, probably talking to Charlie right now. But they're not dating, she told me. She's fine. You are all wrong," I sputtered angrily.

They just kept staring at me, and tears were streaming down my sister's face. My father's eyes had tears, and even my mother looked devastated. My father walked over to me and sat me down in a kitchen chair.

"Maggie, honey, I'm so sorry," my mother walked over to me and put out her arms, but I wouldn't go near her.

"How do you know it's true?" I fired a question at them angrily. I wouldn't back down. I wanted evidence.

My father sighed and pushed his dark hair back on his head. Then he sat down next to me.

"I called Mr. Moran just now when Patty told me what she heard. He confirmed it. The police found her body this morning," my father explained.

Mr. Moran was our neighbor. He wasn't a cop, but he worked in the Tax Office at the Town Hall, where the Police Station was. He knew everything that happened in town.

"Maggie, I wish to God this wasn't true and we didn't have to tell you," my father said, apologizing for the heartbreaking news. I could hear the grief in his voice.

"What happened to her? Did she have an accident?" I asked frantically.

"The police aren't sure, but it looks as if someone hurt her," my father said softly, as if his tone could lessen the horror.

"She was covered with dirt. Someone murdered her," Patty's voice was suddenly eerily calm, like she was in a trance.

"Patty, enough," my mother chided my sister, who just stared at her like a zombie.

"But who would hurt Gina?" I asked my family and the universe. And as the reality of the news started to seep into me, I started to cry. I wanted to get away from them and the horrific words they were saying.

I shot up and shoved Patty out of my way. Then I ran back up to my bedroom and slammed the door. I started to pace. I felt weightless and sick, as if I might float away and evaporate. I wanted to know I was still solid, still real, so I grabbed the violet plant my grandmother had given me for graduation off my desk and smashed it on the floor. The dirt exploded onto my rug.

My mother came into my room. She glanced at the dirt but said nothing. She placed ginger ale and saltines on my nightstand, as if I had the flu. I wouldn't look at her. I got in bed with my back to her, pulling covers up over my head. I was willing her and this new reality to disappear. She gently sat on the side of the bed and sighed.

"Maggie, I'm so sorry. Please try to calm down," she said softly. I could only imagine what all this raw emotion was doing to her. My mother was in her element when fighting, but she despised tears as a weakness and loss of control. She must have felt like screaming herself.

"Please leave. I don't want you here," I choked out. Suddenly I hated her more than I ever had.

"Maggie, I'm not leaving you alone when you are acting like this," she said more firmly, her patience waning.

"I'm not going to jump out the window, if that's what you think," I sneered. "I won't leave an embarrassing mess in your garden," I said sarcastically. Although suddenly, that's exactly what I wanted to do.

"Can you get a hold of yourself?" she asked me pointedly. She sat on my bed woodenly, seeming unsure what to do.

"Yes, I will be fine," I said through gritted teeth. "You don't have to stay here. Please leave," I said angrily.

"It's a terrible thing that has happened, Margaret Grace. I'm so sorry," she said softly, patting my back. My mother never comforted me this way. We rarely even hugged. I couldn't even remember sitting on her lap as a small child.

"Maggie, please look at me," my mother said quietly. But I still wouldn't look at her. Finally, she got up. Before she left my room, she paused at the door.

"You need to stay around the house until they catch this person. No traipsing around the neighborhood," she warned, and I wanted to remind her that she was the one who kicked me out of the house every day to "play like a normal kid." But I didn't want to turn around and see her. I was so angry.

"The police will find who did this. I'll be right downstairs if you need me," she said quietly, but she left my door wide open when she went back downstairs. I got up and slammed it shut again.

I couldn't imagine a world without Gina in it, or anyone who would want to hurt her. I felt so alone and so very frightened.

I got back in bed. I started to cry, and I couldn't stop. None of this made sense. She couldn't be murdered. No one was murdered in our stupid small town. There had to be a mistake. No one would hurt Gina. She was the best person ever. Someone left her there in the trees and dirt. I couldn't bear thinking about it, yet horrific images kept intruding on my thoughts. How could it be that I would never see her again?

A few minutes later, my dad appeared at my door with the newspaper in his hand.

"I'm just going to sit here and read," he announced and sat in my desk chair, unfolding the paper out on my desk. He looked comically large in my small white desk chair, but nothing seemed funny to me anymore, and I wondered if it ever would again.

My father knew better than to try to talk to me. What was there to say? So, he read the paper, and I stayed lying on my bed facing the wall for hours it seemed. I was frozen.

Eventually, I had to use the bathroom. I went through my nightly ritual of brushing my teeth and putting on my nightgown. But my arms and hands were jelly, and everything seemed blurry and underwater.

My father looked up when I came back into my room. He noticed my nightgown.

"Do you think you can sleep?" he asked me, and I shrugged.

I climbed in bed and faced the wall again.

"I'll just stay here until you fall asleep," he said quietly, and I didn't respond.

I was tired and I fell asleep quickly, but the dreams came back. The vampire enveloped me, and I saw Gina walking towards me with dirt and leaves on her. I woke up in a sweat. I was alone in my room, and the light was off. My father must have gone to bed himself. I noticed the dirt from the plant was cleaned up. My mother must have cleaned it while I slept.

I started pacing around my room, repeating the "Our Father" to calm down. I got dizzy, so I sat down on the bench by my window. The night was quiet, but rather than peaceful, it seemed eerie. Somewhere out there on those sleepy streets was a murderer. Was he sleeping, prowling, murdering someone else?

I saw a car drive slowly down the street. It was long and dark, like Father Anthony's car. What would he be doing driving at 2 am in the neighborhood? The car parked at the corner for a while and then drove away suddenly, its tail end swerving around the corner like a serpent.

I crept back into bed and buried myself beneath my covers. The world was a very dark place.

Nothing Makes Sense

Saturday, July 1, 1972

Saturday morning when I awoke, I still couldn't believe Gina was gone. I had a horrible headache, and my mouth was dry from crying so much. I had no desire to watch my cartoons or even eat breakfast. I could hear my mother vacuuming downstairs. She had vacuumed yesterday, so a repeat job could only mean she was still having her bridge night. I couldn't believe it.

Patty knocked on my door and came into my room without waiting for me to answer. She was dressed and had put on makeup, obviously ready to go somewhere.

"I'm going over to Debbie's. Do you want to come with me?" she offered nicely. She never volunteered to take me anywhere. When I was younger, she was forced by our mother, and I suffered for it. But she knew how much I loved Gina, how much we both did. Still, I didn't feel like leaving my room. The only person I wanted to see was Richie, and my mother wouldn't let me do that today.

"That's okay. I think I'm going to just stay here and read or something," I offered back weakly.

"Okay, well I won't be gone that long if you want to talk later or anything. I just want to get out of this dreadful house, as usual," she said dramatically and then smiled at me a bit. She waited for a second, seeming unsure what to say, and then left, shutting the door gently behind her.

I got out *The Wizard of Earthsea* and tried to read, but all I could think about was Gina. Everyone loved her. How could someone do such a horrible thing? The only other person I had ever known who had died was my grandfather who was old and sick, and I wasn't at all sad about that.

But Gina was young and beautiful, and she had so many plans ahead of her. I had asked her once if I could be in her wedding when she got married. I secretly thought she might ask Charlie to be in it, even though girls didn't pick the groomsmen. But if the guy she married liked Charlie (and who didn't?), he might be in the wedding, and we could be paired together. It would be the start of our great romance because I would be older, tall and thin with silky hair. She laughed when I asked, but she pinkie-promised me, and I knew she wouldn't forget me when her big day came. Now it would never come.

I could feel my stomach rumbling, betraying me. I didn't want to leave my room. But eventually, my hunger won, and I went downstairs. I saw the card table set up in the living room, so my mother was definitely having company. Why she didn't just use the dining room table, I didn't know. But I'm sure she had some snooty etiquette rule about it.

As I walked into the kitchen, my mother was drinking a cup of coffee and staring out the window at her garden. She was dressed for the day, in a crisp white blouse and a culotte skirt. My mother never hung around in her pajamas, and I knew she would look disapprovingly at me because I was still in my old yellow nightgown.

"Good morning, Maggie," she said softly.

I shrugged in reply, not wanting to give her the satisfaction of an answer. I knew being angry at her right now was irrational, but I had a lot of anger in me, and my deep resentment of her made her an easy target. It was mean, I knew, but I didn't care.

"How are you today? I hope you were able to sleep," she said with genuine concern.

"Yeah, I did eventually," I reluctantly answered and sighed.

"You have lots of wonderful memories of Gina to comfort you," she advised me, sounding entirely too much like a greeting card. I didn't doubt that my mom was sad in her own way, but her motto in life was to keep moving and never wallow.

"You're still having your party?" I asked with more than a little snip to my voice. Grief made me bold.

"It's not a party. It's just bridge with the Conways. I canceled everyone else. But I thought it would be comforting to see good friends," she explained and put her coffee cup in the dishwasher. It was obvious that the subject was not up for discussion. She had deemed her company appropriate and that was all there was to it.

"Can I see Richie then, for comfort?" I asked sharply. She turned and stared at me.

"I thought I made it clear that it wasn't safe for you to be riding a bike all over town right now," she stated primly. She was becoming irritated with what I am sure she perceived to be impudence on my part. But due to the situation, she was constraining herself and trying to be patient with me.

"Patty went out," I pointed out.

"To see her girlfriend. If you wanted to see a girlfriend, I could drop you off," she added pointedly.

I shrugged. I just didn't have it in me to really take her on. I felt exhausted and weighed down by sadness, a kind of sadness I had not known could exist.

"I need help in my garden, if you are interested?" she was trying to be nice, I could see that. She mostly didn't want any of us, Patty, Dad, or me near her garden. She was positive we would kill every plant. I couldn't think of anything less appealing than digging in the dirt as my mother scolded me to be gentle with flowers that she liked better than me.

"That's okay. I'm going to read," I answered.

She nodded. "Well, at least get dressed. You'll feel better. And if you want to talk, you know where I am," she added and headed out the back screen door to her garden.

As she opened the door, a thought seemed to occur to her.

"You know, talking to Father Anthony might help you," she suggested. As always, the Church was her answer for everything. But I wasn't feeling so happy with God right now.

I didn't respond and she walked out to her garden.

I poured a bowl of Lucky Charms and munched absentmindedly away, reading the back of the box. I remembered a time when Gina had helped me draw the Trix Rabbit for a contest on the back of a cereal box. My drawing skills were awful, but hers were great. She said it was a joint effort, but I could take the credit. I didn't win, but I did get a jumbo glow-in-the-dark sticker of the Trix Rabbit for entering, and the day it came in the mail, I called her up so excited. In retrospect, I'm sure she had forgotten all about it, but she acted like it was a really big deal. The sticker was still stuck to the top of my desk in my bedroom.

I tried Richie on the phone in the kitchen, but the number was busy. I waited a half-hour and tried again, but it was still busy.

I spent the rest of the day in my nightgown, just to annoy my mother. She didn't say anything, but definitely noticed, and there might have been some eye-rolling.

As a custom, when my parents had friends over, my sister and I got Swanson TV dinners. We both loved them, and I could tell my mother was offended by how excited we were for these pre-packaged meals when she cooked for us every day.

My sister always ate the dessert first, cherry cobbler. But I was more of a traditionalist and ate the chicken and potatoes first. Dad bought ice cream for us as a treat because he was feeling bad for us. I felt guilty eating my mint chocolate chip ice cream because I knew he bought it because Gina was dead. Nothing seemed good anymore, not even my favorite ice cream.

Before the Conways arrived, Dad brought up a small TV set he kept in his office to my sister's room, so we could watch TV there. We evacuated the parental area when we heard the Conways ring the doorbell. I never liked gossipy Mrs. Conway, having listened to her skewer Gina and other assorted community members at length on previous bridge nights.

As far as I could tell, there was nothing likable about Mrs. Conway. She was tall and angular, and her squinty eyes always seemed to be drilling me for information. Their son Robby was in Patty's class, and she said he was always making dirty jokes and staring at her chest. But he was an altar boy and a saint in my mother's eyes. Every so often, my mother would hint that Patty should date Robby, and Patty would make an exaggerated gagging sound that was not appreciated.

Patty and I started to watch an old Doris Day movie, the two of us squished together on her bed. She was painting her nails a bright red that my mother would hate and asked if I wanted mine painted. As much as I would have loved to annoy my mother, I just didn't feel like it. A world without Gina seemed gray and colorless, so I might as well be, too.

I thought I heard Mrs. Conway say Gina's name, so I crept to the top of the stairs to listen. Patty joined me sitting on the top stair a moment later. We both knew to stay silent.

"Well, Gina was always kind of a wild child. The hippie stuff, the protests, the boyfriends. No father and that's what happens. I know Anita tried with her, but she was never firm with that girl," she lectured. Mrs. Conway was talking with her usual air of absolute certainty.

I felt myself becoming furious at her depiction of Gina, and her mother who was so sweet. Mrs. Conway didn't even know Gina.

"Carol, Gina was a lovely girl when she was younger. I wouldn't have let her watch the girls if she wasn't," my mother said, and I could imagine my mother's stern smile. Mrs. Conway was treading on dangerous ground.

"Well, then she changed. I mean, what was she doing on Pirate's Island at night? No good even comes from that spot. They should chop all those trees down," Mrs. Conway squawked this fact out with tremendous indignation.

Gina would never be there on purpose, especially at night.

"And then she was always with that colored boy," Mrs. Conway continued her dissection of Gina's flaws, as if her murder was the obvious outcome of her behavior. I wanted to scream at her that lots of people in our town, including her stupid son, behaved really badly and they didn't get murdered for it.

"The Harpers are a good family, Carol," my dad piped up, defending Richie's family. I wished he would use some blasphemous expletives to correct Mrs. Conway, but somehow my dad could always control his temper with people outside the family.

Mrs. Conway snorted in contempt, "Well, Tom, I know you and I don't agree on *that* issue," she countered.

"We have raised our children not to see color, but look at character," my mother snapped back, in an absurd paraphrase of Reverend Martin Luther King. The hypocrisy of it made my eyes roll back in my head. It was true she did not say overtly racist things to me about Richie, but I knew exactly how she felt about him.

"And she was pregnant, too. I heard she was in counseling with Father Anthony, trying to sort that mess out. These girls today run wild, and then the parents wonder why these things happen," Mrs. Conway continued her self-righteous damnation of Gina.

My mother wasn't one to take a slight like that. "You have sons, Carol. You have no idea what it's like to raise daughters. We have to worry about a lot more than you do," she retorted crisply, and I'm sure her comment was accompanied by a blistering stare.

"Well, Vivian, I'm sure Patty and Margaret are nothing like Gina. You are their role model, not some babysitter," Mrs. Conway managed to get in a jab in the form of a compliment. She knew how much time we had spent with Gina as kids. I bet my mother was regretting having this bridge night after all.

Mr. Conway piped up finally to change the subject, obviously irritated with his wife's miserable monologue. He was a large man, with a big round belly and thick glasses. Mr. Conway had always been nice to me, although he never got my name right. "Hello, Martha," he would say with a smile.

"Are you still planning to vote for McGovern, Tom?" Mr. Conway veered towards politics, and my mother started talking about her garden with Mrs. Conway, but I could hear a snip in my mother's voice that evidenced she wouldn't be forgetting Mrs. Conway's insults any time soon.

Patty pulled my arm and motioned me back upstairs to her room. She shut the door and pulled me to sit down on the bed.

"You can't tell anyone what we heard," she cautioned me.

"Why? What part?" I asked.

"All of it. The pregnant part, the Father Anthony part. Carol Conway is a nasty, gossipy pig who raised a pervert. I don't trust anything she says. I don't care if Mom thinks she's a good person because of all the stuff she does at church and school. All that crap she said was wrong and mean," my sister's voice quivered with anger.

"I won't tell. I don't believe it anyway. And Gina wasn't wild," I added firmly.

"So, what if she was? We loved her, and she loved us, and that's all that matters," Patty reasoned. And I wondered then if Patty knew things about Gina I didn't know.

We sat on her bed for a minute and watched Doris Day marry Rock Hudson in the movie.

"Why can't life be like that?" she asked, and I shrugged. I had never understood life less.

"The problem is Carol Conway has probably blabbed that all over town already," she said with a sudden sad realization. I knew she was right.

"Do you really think Gina was pregnant? She broke up with Ray. Why would she do that if she was pregnant?" I asked, confused by everything.

"Who knows?" Patty said with a sigh.

"Well, if anyone says anything about Gina to me, I will fight them," I threatened in my squeaky voice.

"Easy, Mags. We can't really do anything about any of this," she cautioned me, well aware that my social status was already on the lowest rung possible.

But I didn't agree. I didn't know what I would do, but I knew I had to do something.

A Family of Strangers

Sunday, July 2, 1972

My mother got me up for church in the morning. I would have protested, but I was too depressed to muster the energy it would take. It had only been two days since I found out Gina was dead, and it felt like months. Time had slowed to a torturous crawl, and I still hadn't been able to see Richie or even talk to him on the phone. His phone line was perpetually busy, and my mother hadn't let me go to his house.

The four of us sat at breakfast in silence. My dad only had coffee, and I suspected he was hungover. He usually drank quite a bit to weather my mother's social plans. My sister and I munched a bit on dry cereal and looked absentmindedly at the Sunday comics. But the Peanuts just made me sad because it was Gina's and my favorite.

My mother stood up and rinsed out her coffee cup and attempted to get us moving.

"I think Mass is what we all need the most right now," she advised sternly. We all rose reluctantly and drove to church in silence.

Outside church, people were whispering in clusters, and I was sure Gina was the topic of every conversation. I wondered if these churchgoers would be any kinder in their comments about Gina than Mrs. Conway had been.

Church seemed more morose than usual, even though it wasn't a funeral Mass, just regular Sunday service. I stared at the sun gleaming through the stained-glass windows and tried to picture Gina in some kind of heaven.

Father Anthony gave a trembling homily about how God will comfort us in time of need. He never mentioned Gina directly, but it was clear he was attempting to reassure the congregation that God was with us. But all I felt was anger.

Why hadn't God been with Gina and saved her? He had let her down when she needed Him most. As Mass continued, I said the prayers I had memorized long ago, but I didn't feel close to God at all. And Father Anthony provided me with no comfort. After seeing what looked like Father Anthony's car driving around the neighborhood in the middle of the night, all I got was a spooky feeling from him. He seemed part of the dark landscape of the night where bad things happened.

On the way home from Mass, I tried to think of anyone who would want to hurt Gina. I thought of Ray and his desperation Thursday night to find her. Would he kill her out of revenge because she ditched him? It seemed unthinkable.

I knew old Mr. Feeney didn't like Gina because she had protested the Vietnam War downtown. He shouted at her that she was a "disrespectful hippie," but she just smiled and waved. I remember once when my dad was watching the news about riots, he said that the most dangerous people were the ones with nothing to lose.

I didn't know what he meant then, but I thought of Mr. Feeney. He had lost his son, his wife, and he was so angry. But was he dangerous? It was hard to picture Mr. Feeney having the strength to kill anyone. He was mostly just a little troll, shouting at people who passed by his house. But he did seem crazy, so who knows what he might do.

After church, we skipped Grandma's house because Grandma and Uncle Jimmy were coming over for dinner later. Even though my mother forbade it, I decided to ride my bike to Richie's house. She was so busy preparing dinner that she probably wouldn't even realize I was gone. As long as I was back in my room by dinner time, it would be fine.

I ditched the dorky dress with the babyish Peter Pan collar that my mother made me wear to church, and I put on my shorts and a t-shirt. Then, I tiptoed out the front door and around the side of the house to my bike. I pedaled away as fast as I could.

I arrived at Richie's house and knocked softly on the screen door. Monica appeared, looking very sad.

"Hey Maggie May," she said softly, and it occurred to me that I would never hear Gina call me that again.

"Hi Monica," I answered and gave her a sad wave.

She called for Richie, then stepped outside to the front porch.

"I'm so sorry about Gina. We all loved her," she said and hugged me tight. I could feel the lump in my throat that meant tears were coming.

"Thanks," I said, empty of any words. Instead, I looked down at my old sneakers. They were dirty, and one of the laces had a permanent knot I couldn't get out. My mom would have said I looked scrappy.

Richie pushed past Monica and dragged me down the steps onto the sidewalk.

He started to cry, and I rubbed his back as we sat on the concrete.

"She was the best person, Maggie," he looked at me, his face streaked with tears.

"I know she was," I agreed with him.

"Charlie's really upset. I think maybe he was in love with her. He took off all day yesterday, and when he came home, he wouldn't talk to anyone," he explained softly.

We sat in silence for a while, and it was comforting just to be near him. After a time, we started to play hopscotch just to pass the time, but neither of us cared much if we landed on the squares or not.

After an hour or so, Richie's mother called him in for supper, so I had to go home. I wished I could have stayed there for supper, but I knew I couldn't with Grandma and Uncle Jimmy arriving soon. Richie and I never had formal goodbyes, just parted with a wave, but this time he hugged me tight.

"You're my best friend, Maggie," he whispered in my ear.

"You, too," I whispered back.

"Be careful riding home. Watch out for monsters," he warned me, and I felt our deep connection. He knew me; he even knew things I had never said out loud.

I rode my bike home as fast as I could. Richie was right. Even in the daylight, nothing seemed safe anymore.

By the time I arrived at home, I saw Grandma and Uncle Jimmy's car in the driveway. There was no way to get to my bedroom and pretend I had been home the whole time, but I did manage to sneak my bike back to the side of the house. At least that way, I could just pretend I had only been out on our street. I trudged up the steps, wondering if this once Grandma would refrain from frowning at my outfit. She didn't.

"Hello Maggie," she said morosely, then looked me over with her customary disappointment, gave me a quick hug, and attempted to smooth my hair with both hands. She paused and looked at me again, and then I saw her lick her hand to fix my hair like I was a baby, but I ducked, and she gave up.

"Hi Grandma, Uncle Jimmy," I gave them obligatory greetings. Uncle Jimmy just nodded. He was too busy gobbling down cashews my mom had placed on the coffee table to actually speak.

He looked so large and ridiculous sitting on her floral sofa, knees banging up against the coffee table. I would have laughed if I wasn't so sad. I wondered if he would get scolded for all the crumbs he was creating, but somehow, I doubted it.

Patty was sitting at one end of the sofa, as far from Uncle Jimmy as possible. She looked miserable, and we exchanged commiserating glances. Then Patty held her nose and gestured to Uncle Jimmy, and I had to stifle a laugh. Luckily no one else saw.

My mother entered the room in a starched blue dress with a forced smile and announced, "Dinner is ready." She motioned to us to sit down. She didn't address my afternoon's absence, and I wondered if she was secretly quite relieved that my tangible grief and I were gone for a while. However, she did stop me from sitting down and directed me to the bathroom.

"Clean up first. We are eating in the dining room," she chastised me, and I pondered why eating one room over from the kitchen affected the required level of cleanliness. It was humiliating because I certainly knew enough to clean up before dinner. But perhaps this was my punishment for leaving without telling her.

My mother had set the dining room table with good China, and I saw that she had prepared a Sunday roast with mashed potatoes, Uncle Jimmy's favorite.

My mother said grace, and we all mumbled along. Then, she attempted to keep the dinner conversation light by talking about her garden, flowers, and the weather, but Jimmy opened his big mouth.

"Shame about the Russo girl," he said, hulked over his plate, his mouth sputtering out mashed potatoes. I just stared at him.

Grandma chimed in, "It certainly is. Have to keep a close eye on girls these days," she added and nodded toward Patty and me. Patty kicked my leg under the table, and when I looked at her, she rolled her eyes. I bristled at Grandma, because it seemed she, like Mrs. Conway, was blaming Gina for being murdered.

"Edna, I'm sure you know boys can get in as much trouble as girls, if not more," my father shot back at Grandma sharply, looking directly at her, then glancing at Uncle Jimmy, and she paled at his remark. My mother glared at him for reprimanding her mother.

"Well, our girls are not running around at all, Mom. We keep them reined in," my mother reassured Grandma that we were well under control, like some kind of livestock.

"She sure was a pretty girl. The Russo girl. Beautiful girl. I mean really beautiful," Jimmy continued to shove food in his mouth and simultaneously talk to no one in particular. He never really said anything, so his verbosity on the subject struck me as strange and offensive.

Gina was pretty, but she was so much more than that. Did it only matter when pretty girls were murdered? I remembered then that Gina had once asked me if Uncle Jimmy ever babysat us. I laughed at the notion and said, "No, he's too lazy," a descriptor I had gotten from my father, who referred to Jimmy as my mother's "goddamn lazy brother." But Gina didn't laugh. She just said, "Good. Make sure he never does."

Looking at Jimmy now, his sweaty face, jowls moving as he aggressively chewed, he reminded me of an ogre from a fairy tale. And I wondered how many high school girls he ogled while he stalked about the high school with his broom. I suddenly felt afraid of him. Was he more like my grandfather than I thought?

My father changed the subject to politics. My dad was a Democrat, but my grandmother was decidedly more conservative, and I saw my mother shoot my father another death stare. But he was definitely a few drinks in, so he ignored her and began pontificating on why George McGovern should be President.

Uncle Jimmy stared perplexedly at my father as if he was speaking in tongues, and I wondered how my mother could be so arrogant when her brother was such a complete moron. Grandma ignored Dad and started up the garden conversation again. I asked to be excused as soon as possible.

Patty and I both went upstairs. She came into my room and started looking at my 45's.

"You okay?" she asked me, eyeing me from the side as she browsed the records.

"Not really. You?" I asked. She shook her head.

"Everyone loved Gina. It just doesn't make any sense. Who would want to hurt her?" I asked.

"Debbie's brother says it was probably some guy just going through town. He says there are serial killers who just go all over the country. He says the guy is probably a hundred miles away by now," Patty offered this as if it would be reassuring.

But it didn't make sense, and it certainly didn't make me feel any better for Gina to be randomly killed by some psycho just passing through town.

"I'm going to figure it out," I said with determination.

"Mags, calm down," she stared at me. "You're not a cop," she pointed out unnecessarily.

But I didn't argue because she was trying to be nice. She stared at herself in my mirror.

"Do you think I would look good as a redhead?" she asked. "I think dyeing my hair might cheer me up, and it will piss off Mom so that's the added bonus," she poked me to get a laugh.

"You'd look great as a redhead," I answered.

"We could do yours too and really make her flip," she grinned wickedly.

"No thanks," I answered, thinking that the only thing worse than out of control curly brown hair would be out of control curly red hair. Imagine the teasing that would provoke. I could hear the Bozo the Clown jokes already. I would stay as invisible as possible.

That night before bed, I arranged my dolls and stuffed animals around me, and I pulled out my journal. I made a list of potential suspects: Ray, Mr. Feeney, then after hesitating, I added Uncle Jimmy at the end. I hid it under my mattress and willed myself to go to sleep. I said my prayers, and I promised Gina I would find out who did this.

I prayed for a dreamless sleep.

Betrayal

Monday, July 3, 1972

I woke up late Monday, after a night of unsettling dreams. I was running, and Gina was just out of reach. It was dark, and there were strange people in the shadows. I was relieved it was morning and I was awake in the solid world of daytime. I was determined to find out who hurt Gina, and I needed my best friend to help me, so I was heading to Richie's house.

I tiptoed downstairs for breakfast, pouring some Lucky Charms into a plastic bag and drinking a glass of water. My mother was outside in her garden, my dad at work, and Patty off somewhere with friends, I figured. I wanted to leave before my mother could ask where I was going.

I got my bike from the side of the house and hollered goodbye to my mom over the fence. As she turned to look at me, I jumped on my bike and pedaled as fast as I could. I would probably pay for it later, but at least she couldn't say she didn't know I left.

I arrived at Richie's house, relieved to see Charlie's car in the driveway. I could sure use a Charlie hug right now.

I dropped my bike on the lawn and padded up the steps of the front porch. I peered through the screen door, and I waved at Grandma Rose. She came slowly over to the door, but she didn't open it and welcome me in.

"Hey Grandma Rose," I gave her a smile. She looked sadly down at me. I wanted her to hug me. I wanted the comfort I could not find in my own house.

"Hello, Maggie. I'm afraid it's not a good day for you to be here. I think you had better go home. I'm sorry," she said softly. And then she shut the solid wood front door.

I stood there, stunned. I felt as if someone had slapped me. She said it gently, but I felt pain in my chest.

I was still standing on the front porch in shock when Richie came around from the garage. I ran off the steps to catch him.

"Richie, Richie!" I called, but he just stood on the sidewalk, staring at me.

"What's going on? Grandma Rose shut the door in my face," I gasped, nearly in tears, my heart was racing.

Richie stood staring at the hopscotch board we had drawn on the sidewalk yesterday.

"Richie, what is it?" I started to panic, thinking someone else had died.

"The police took Charlie this morning to ask him questions about Gina's murder," he said flatly, still not looking at me.

"Why? Do they think Charlie could help?" I asked, thinking Charlie probably knew more about Gina's life than we did.

"No, Maggie. He's a suspect," Richie said, anger tinging his voice.

"What? That's crazy!! Charlie would never hurt anyone!" I protested.

"When your dad dropped me off Thursday night, Charlie and Gina were going somewhere, and your dad saw them," he stated coldly.

"So? They are friends. I don't understand," I sputtered.

"Your parents called the police. Charlie was the last person someone saw Gina with," he looked me straight in the eye.

"What are you talking about?" I asked, my mouth agape in confusion.

"You parents reported Charlie to the police. As a suspect. The police picked him up," Richie explained stoically.

The reality hit me. I felt dizzy and my chest hurt. My parents called the police. On Charlie. My parents, who had known Charlie since he was a kid, knew he would never hurt anyone. I just stared at Richie.

"Richie, I…" I had no words.

"You'd better go. My dad and Charlie are still at the police station. My mom wants me inside," he said flatly and walked away, up the steps and back into his house, closing the door behind him.

I stood on the sidewalk for a few minutes, trying to absorb the fact that I was no longer welcome at their house. My family had betrayed his. Charlie was at the police station. And Richie, my best friend, had rejected me. There was nowhere safe for me to go.

I took off on my bike, going nowhere in particular. I thought about the fact that the only reason I knew how to ride a bike was because of Gina and Charlie. I was hopeless when my dad first took my training wheels off because of fear and my fundamental lack of coordination. My dad tried to teach me, but with my mother standing on the front lawn watching critically, I floundered.

Then one day when Gina was at Richie's house hanging out with Charlie, she decided I would learn. With Gina and Charlie on either side of my bike, I finally got the hang of it. As I pedaled down the street, I could hear them hooting and hollering, cheering me on.

The more I thought about Gina's murder and what was now happening to Charlie, the angrier I became. I was crying and pedaling furiously. I wasn't even really watching where I was going, and a car honked its horn at me by the school when I rode across traffic.

I took off down the bike paths by the school. I wanted to see Pirates Island, where it had happened. I could see the yellow police tape through the trees. A soccer team was practicing on the field as if there wasn't a murder scene 50 feet away. Didn't anyone care? Bitterly, I thought that the school should have cut the trees down years ago, and then Gina might still be alive.

When I got to the other end of the bike path, I rode through the streets of my town, fueled by fury. All these stupid, lousy people mowing their lawns and talking to neighbors, and the very best person in town had been murdered. But they had reduced Gina to a snippet of gossip, instead of the living, breathing person she was. When I couldn't pedal any further, and my legs felt like rubber, I headed home.

My father's car was in the driveway when I arrived, earlier than usual. I burst through the front door, brave with rage and grief.

My parents were sitting in the living room, drinks in hand, reading the evening newspaper. I knew I must have looked crazy, tears on my face and my hair all crazy and big from sweat and the wind from the bike.

"How could you do this?" I pointed a shaking finger at my parents.

"What are you talking about, Margaret Grace? And don't you use that tone with me," my mother snapped back, lowering her newspaper to look me up and down, taking in my disheveled appearance with a roll of her eyes.

"You told the police Charlie was with Gina! Charlie would never hurt anyone. You know Charlie. How could you do that to him? To his family?" I could feel my voice quaking. I had never stood up to my parents this way before. Patty walked into the room and stared at me like I'd lost my mind.

My father stuffed his newspaper in the magazine stand beside his chair and stood up. He walked toward me slowly, as if he was cornering a rabid raccoon. "Maggie, calm down. Your mother just felt we had a responsibility to report what we knew, so she called," he explained.

"Of course, it was you," I sneered at my mother. "You ruin everything!" I had never felt such anger.

"You will not talk to me this way. You will be respectful," my mother commanded coldly and stood up. Then she neatly folded her newspaper—creasing it like origami—and placed it on the coffee table. Her concern about the tidiness of her house right now infuriated me.

"Charlie's innocent. He wouldn't hurt anyone ever. You know that!" I screamed at her.

"That's for the police to decide, Maggie," my mother said sternly, and I realized she suspected Charlie.

I was dumbstruck. Charlie was only 19. When had he become this dangerous man in my mother's mind?

"You have known Charlie since he was a little kid, and he is the sweetest person in the world," I continued to defend him.

"Charlie and Gina were seen at the diner in town on Thursday night. Gina was crying. We aren't the only people who reported seeing them together," my mother informed me sharply.

"No, you just had to be the first! He was probably trying to help her. They are friends," I shot back fiercely.

"Well, the police may have a different interpretation," she quipped snidely.

"They don't know Charlie like we do!" I said through gritted teeth.

"You are to stay away from Richie from now on. That's final," she added gravely.

"Well, that won't be a problem. Because of you, I'm not welcome there anymore!" I howled.

"That's for the best!" she snapped.

"No, it's not. He's my best friend!" I yelled at her in defiance. My body was alive with rage.

"That's it, Margaret Grace. I understand you are very sad, but I will not tolerate this insolence. I'm making you an appointment to talk with Father Anthony. You need someone to help you with all this anger," she announced in a condescending tone, throwing her hands up as if I was beyond help.

A thought suddenly struck me. Freaky Father Anthony!

"Oh my God, it's probably Father Anthony! He probably did it, got her pregnant, and then he murdered her to cover it up! He's weird, always driving around the neighborhood at night! I saw him handing out baseball cards to kids, and then one night when I got up in the middle of the night, I saw his car from my bedroom window, driving down the street. I knew there was something wrong with him! We could go to the police and tell them, and they'd know it wasn't Charlie," I got excited by my revelation.

The next thing I knew, my mother slapped my face, her own face red with outrage.

I held my hand to my cheek to calm the stinging. I was shocked into silence.

"How dare you make such an accusation about a priest! He was trying to help Gina!" she hissed at me, her hands shaking, and then turned away from me and faced the coffee table.

Suddenly, I hated that stupid coffee table and her stupid floral sofa. I kicked the coffee table as hard as I could, startling her from behind. When she turned around, she looked genuinely shocked.

"That's enough, Maggie." My father put his arm in front of me as if I was a danger to my mother.

"You don't know anything. You don't see anything the way it is!" I felt myself losing control.

"No, Maggie. You don't know anything. You are the one who lives in a fantasy world," my mother stated coldly, pity in her voice.

"Wrong. You don't even see that your own brother is a creep, talking about how pretty Gina was, when she's dead!" I yelled, words tumbling out of me. I was crying now.

My mother's eyes grew wide with rage. I hated her at that moment.

"You didn't even know your own father was a creep!" I sneered at her, and she raised her hand, but before she could slap me again, I ran up the stairs, slammed my door, and locked it.

Downstairs, I could hear my parents fighting.

"You need to deal with her!" my mother yelled at my father, the word "her" dripping with contempt.

"What's she talking about with your father?" my father demanded angrily.

My mother didn't answer. So, my father spoke up again, "Vivian, answer me!" he insisted.

"She's making things up. She's angry with me. She wants to punish me. How should I know?" my mother's voice shook in fury and panic.

"It doesn't sound like nothing," my father shot back bitterly. Then there was silence for a moment. The silence scared me the most.

"My father was a wonderful man," my mother asserted fiercely, but her voice was fighting through tears now. I wondered if even my mother believed what she was saying.

I heard the front screen door slam, and I assumed my father had walked outside to get away from her.

I had heard enough anyway. I didn't want to listen to my mother call me a liar, yet in some weird way I felt guilty for speaking the truth. The thought of them discussing what I said made me panicked and queasy. I turned on my record player, put on "Alone Again Naturally" and set it to repeat. Because I was. Chubby, wild-haired, pants-peeing, loser me. Alone again. I had lost Gina, Charlie would hate me, and now I was losing Richie.

I put my head between two pillows, so I wouldn't hear anything from downstairs. I don't know how long I stayed that way. I was exhausted from anger and loss. Eventually, I fell asleep.

It was dark out when I woke up.

I heard my mother coming up the stairs and braced myself for her to start yelling at me again. But instead, she unlocked my door with a screwdriver and stood in the doorway for a minute. From a space in between my pillows, I could see her, screwdriver in hand, walk over and unplug the record player. The record slurred to a halt. But she didn't come near me.

"Never speak about my father again," she said flatly. Then she turned and left, shutting the door quietly behind her.

I lay awake for a long time, feeling as if the world had fallen off its axis and was hurtling wildly through space. I was dizzy. All I could do was hold onto my dolls and hope I didn't fall off.

Independence Day

Tuesday, July 4, 1972

When I woke up Tuesday morning, still in my clothes from yesterday, the house was silent. I looked in the backyard, but my mother wasn't in her garden. I crept out of my room and knocked on my sister's door.

Patty opened her door and sat back down on her bed. As usual, she was brushing her hair.

"Hey," I said.

"You okay?" she asked me.

"I guess," I said with a shrug. My head was pounding. I imagined this was how a hangover must feel.

"You went batshit last night. For real. Mom was psycho mad," she remarked. "It was like scary." She stared at me, eyes narrowed, as if to assess if I had regained my senses.

"Where is she?" I whispered.

"Not sure. She left this morning. Maybe she went to Grandma's," she guessed. I hoped she wouldn't tell Grandma what I said about Uncle Jimmy and my grandfather.

I stood there, frozen on Patty's pink rug, wondering what to do, wondering how I would ever face my own mother again.

"Mags, are you sure you're okay? You look strange," she eyed me with concern.

"I don't know what I am. But I don't want to be here when she gets home," I confessed nervously.

"What did you mean about Grandpa?" Patty questioned me, staring intently. But I had no desire to answer her.

"Nothing. I was just mad," I lied.

She paused, seeming to mull something over in her mind. Then whatever it was, she decided to let it go.

"Want to go to the Town Pool with me today? It's the Fourth of July, remember?" she offered in a moment of sisterly kindness.

I couldn't care less that it was the stupid Fourth of July, and I didn't really want to put on my ugly lemon bathing suit again and show up where my skinny classmates would be in their bikinis, but it was my best chance to escape the house. I literally had nowhere else to go.

"Sure, thanks," I smiled weakly at her.

"Okay, meet you downstairs in like ten minutes," she smiled and returned to brushing her hair.

I ran back to my room, and put on the lemon bathing suit, along with an ugly floral terry cloth cover-up that looked like something my grandmother would wear. Who cared how I looked anyway? My life was ruined.

Patty and I quickly downed some Honeycombs and left a note for our mother on the refrigerator door. "At Town Pool. Be back by dinner. P and M." I wondered if my mother would be angry or relieved that we were gone when she returned home.

We mounted our bikes, towels in our baskets, and took off on the 15-minute ride to the Town Pool. I loved the Town Pool when I was little, still unaware that I was chubby. I could swim by myself, and the other kids more or less ignored me. But now I was far too aware of their unforgiving stares, the way they looked at me with pity and judgment. My plan was to stay with Patty and her 16-year-old friends, and that way, my own peers might leave me alone.

Patty paid our 50-cent admission fees, and we pushed through the turnstiles into the pool area. The Town Pool was really a constellation of pools, including a big Olympic-sized pool where the teenagers dove and hung out, a smaller pool everyone called the "Mom Pool," and a kiddie pool for toddlers. There was also a snack bar.

The pool was decorated for the Fourth with flags, and red, white, and blue balloons were tied all along the fence behind the chaises by the "Mom Pool" and the kiddie pool. I knew they were planning fireworks later because Gina had mentioned going. Now she would never see fireworks again.

I could hear the song "Magic" by Pilot blaring through the pool sound system. "Whoa ho ho, it's magic, you know, never believe it's not so." I thought I sure could use some magic right now.

Patty waved to her friends as we arrived at the big pool. Her best friend Debbie had saved her a lounge chair, but she obviously didn't expect me to be tagging along. People often thought Debbie and my sister were twins because Debbie also was thin with long brown hair, and they shared clothes. I noticed Debbie was wearing one of Patty's old bikinis today. Debbie definitely looked more like Patty than I did. At times, I really did wonder where I came from.

Before Debbie could apologize, I spoke up. "I'll just put my towel on the concrete. It's fine." I forced a smile. My sister sat in the chair and began applying Coppertone to bake herself. She would burn; she had inherited our dad's fair Irish skin. But there was no point in reminding her.

"Here, take off your cover-up and put some on," she handed me the Coppertone. I hesitated.

"Maggie, you look ridiculous with that hideous terry cloth thing on in ninety-degree heat. Don't be a weirdo," she chastised me. I very reluctantly took off my cover-up and put some lotion on my shoulders.

I was doing a scan of the crowd through my sunglasses, and I saw a bunch of kids from my class, boys and girls, playing together in the pool. They were half horsing around, half flirting, and I felt a million miles from them and their world. I wondered when, if ever, I would fit in with my classmates. Would I ever be that effortlessly social, blending in with the crowd, happy, and pretty, and light?

Kids lined up for the high diving board. You had to be 10 years old to use the high dive. The summer I was 10, I decided I was up to the challenge, and I waited in the twisty line for a chance to jump. The line even went up the ladder to the diving board itself, so as each person dove, you were one step on the ladder closer to the top. I was so excited to jump and show my mother and Patty I could do it.

But when I finally got to the top and walked to the edge of the diving board, I froze. All I could think of was how Timmy Constantine had attempted a cannonball the week before and hit the water with such speed that his knees smashed into his teeth, knocking the front two out. The water was all bloody, and the lifeguard had to dive in and pull him out. They never found the teeth as far as I knew.

That day as I looked down at the water, all I remembered was the blood, and I imagined those lost teeth floating around in the depths of the pool. I couldn't do it, so I had to go back down the ladder, which meant everyone else on the ladder had to go back down too. They booed me, and I walked back to my mother and sister, head hung low. Patty rolled her eyes, and all my mother said was, "I don't know what you were thinking," and then she resumed reading her book. Another triumphant moment in the life of Maggie.

I looked toward the Mom Pool, and I spied Monica sitting alone, a safe distance from the rest of her peers. Sitting with her, looking gloomy, was Richie. I wanted so badly to go over there, but I didn't know if I could. Would they reject me? Did they hate me now? I sat on my towel, feeling the sun beat down on my shoulders which were likely already burning. Richie was my best friend. I had to try, so I decided to be brave and face the throngs of people.

"I'm going to walk around," I told my sister. She squinted at me, her hand attempting to shield her eyes. She was in full bake mode.

"Okay. Just don't disappear," she reminded me. It was unusual for my sister to be protective of me, and I figured she must have been more worried about Gina's murder and the prospect of a killer in our midst than she let on.

I nodded in agreement, threw my cover-up back on, and took off.

Monica saw me approaching first, and to my great relief, she smiled and waved. Then Richie looked up.

"Hey," I said sheepishly.

"Hey, Maggie May," she smiled at me. "Give me a hug," she pulled me over and hugged me. I started to cry. She smelled like cocoa butter and kindness.

"This isn't your fault. We know that. It's just real complicated right now," she reassured me.

"I'm so sorry. I hate my mother," I choked on tears.

"Don't say that. It's just not a good time at our house. Everyone is very upset. I brought Richie here for a little while to give Charlie and my parents some space," she tried to explain.

Richie was staring at me, still silent. He was wearing his red swimming trunks with an oversized Jimi Hendrix t-shirt that I knew was Charlie's. I was afraid he would never speak to me again.

Monica dug in her bag and pulled out some dollar bills. "Why don't you two get a snack together?" she nudged Richie with her foot. He reluctantly stood up and we walked off together.

"Please talk to me, Richie. I'm so sorry," I pleaded with him.

He sighed, "I'm not really mad at you, Maggie. It's just that everything is so awful right now. Charlie is so depressed. He isn't really even talking. My parents are arguing, and my grandma cries all the time. What if they arrest him and send him to prison? What if I never see him again?" he sounded despondent.

"We won't let that happen," I promised him with conviction, and he shrugged. But I was committed to fixing everything; after all, my family had been the first to put Charlie under suspicion.

We got in line at the snack bar, and I couldn't think of anything to say. Richie was sullen and sad, all the happy energy let out of him like air from a deflated balloon.

We ordered fries and root beers, and I smothered the fries in ketchup the way Richie liked them. They were usually soggy, so it didn't matter.

Most of the picnic tables were crowded with groups of kids, laughing and chatting in wet bathing suits, or parents attempting to wipe ketchup off wriggling toddlers' faces. We found a picnic table far from the other people and sat down.

I plopped the fries in the center of the table and started to fill Richie in on my plans.

"Listen, Richie, I have a list of suspects that we need to investigate," I explained, and he looked up at me to see if I was kidding or just crazy.

"Maggie, the police say they have all this evidence," he explained. "My dad says they will convict him just because he's Black," he imitated his dad's deep voice when he said it.

"But not if we can prove it's someone else," I asserted defiantly. I pounded my fist on the table, and I saw Richie laugh a little.

"Maggie, you're crazy," he added, rolling his eyes. He finally picked up a French fry and munched on it.

"But a good kind of crazy, right?" I wanted reassurance.

"Yes, the best kind," he complied.

We ate in contented silence for a few minutes, and the sound of Richie slurping his root beer through his straw was music to my ears.

Just as we started to feel a bit like our old selves, three girls from my class strolled by, and I could feel them notice us. They stopped in their tracks.

"Well, if it isn't Mr. and Mrs. Freak," Lydia sneered. I noticed she had sprouted a new pimple on her forehead.

"Shut up, Lydia." I felt brave wanting to protect Richie. The last thing he needed was mean Catholic school girls teasing him right now.

"I can't believe you're still hanging out with him when his brother is a murderer," she dragged out the syllables of murderer to make it sound as horrible as possible, disgust dripping from her voice. Obviously, the news of Charlie's questioning had circulated through our gossipy little town.

"Charlie had nothing to do with what happened to Gina, and I will prove it." I stood up in defiance. They all laughed in a cackling chorus of ridicule.

"Oh my God, you are such a loser," Lydia laughed in disgust. "You two deserve each other. My mother says if you lay down with dogs, you'll get fleas," she commented, her nose in the air.

"But which one of them is the dog?" another girl screeched, and they all fell on each other laughing.

"Maybe Maggie's colored too. After all, she has an afro!" Lydia mocked me. "Maybe you're adopted, Maggie. Even your colored family didn't want you," she jeered.

I could feel a lump in my throat and willed myself not to cry. I was mortified hearing these cruel girls say these racist things in front of Richie.

"Just go away. You are a witch, Lydia. Go pop your giant zit! You're all witches," I hissed at them. Richie was still as a statue, staring at the two soggy fries left in the cardboard tray.

"Fine, we will leave you two colored lovebirds to yourselves," Lydia heckled. I looked up at her. The sunlight made her squint her eyes as she threw head back in an evil cackle. She had never looked uglier.

The girls sauntered away, intentionally laughing extra loud so we could hear them.

"Don't listen to them, Richie. They are witches. Lots of people hate them. I even think the nuns hate them," I tried to make him feel better.

"It's not just them. No one will talk to my parents in the grocery store, anywhere. People are canceling jobs at my dad's garage. No white people will even say hi to my grandma on our street," he explained wearily.

I felt bitterly ashamed of everyone I knew. They had always acted as if they were better people than this. Going to church, Catholic school, but none of it mattered if they could be this hateful. They had all known Charlie forever, and they all knew he wasn't capable of hurting anyone. But to them, he wasn't Charlie anymore. He was suddenly a stranger – a Black man who was seen with a white girl who was murdered. And they drew hideous conclusions.

"I think we need to start investigating suspects," I told him.

"Who are your suspects?" Richie asked me.

"First, there's Ray because Gina had just dumped him, and he seems kind of dangerous. Plus, on Thursday, before you got to my house, he was on our street looking for Gina. He asked if I knew where she was, and he seemed really angry. Maybe he was so angry, he did it," I began. I still couldn't bring myself to say the word murdered or killed."

Richie looked up in thought and then nodded in agreement.

"People are saying Gina was pregnant," I whispered, as I squashed a fry in the ketchup.

"I know. I heard that too," Richie said softly. We got quiet for a moment, not knowing how to feel about that piece of information.

But I had to find answers. Gina deserved answers, so did Charlie.

"Father Anthony at our church is another suspect. Gina was in counseling with him, and he's spooky. He drives around our neighborhood at night talking to kids, and once I saw him driving around the neighborhood in the middle of the night. I'm sure it was his car," I continued.

Richie's eyes grew wide at my inclusion of a priest on the suspect list.

"I know, he's a priest. But there's something weird about him. We're not accusing him. Just investigating him," I explained.

"Okay," he said reluctantly.

"The next one is tough for me," I took a deep breath. "My Uncle Jimmy," I said with a loud exhale.

"What, Maggie???? Your uncle?" he looked at me as if I was crazy.

"Listen, he works at the high school, he knew Gina, and at Sunday dinner at my house, he was blabbing on and on about how beautiful she was. It was super gross. He's like really old, like 45," I explained, my voice dripping with disgust.

"Still, I don't know. He's your uncle," Richie countered me.

"Remember what I told you after roller skating?" I whispered, even though there was no one nearby now. Richie nodded solemnly.

"Well, my grandfather was creepy, so it wouldn't surprise me if Uncle Jimmy was too," I confessed.

Richie looked at me, eyes full of sympathy. But he didn't ask any questions. He took me at my word.

"Finally, there's Mr. Feeney," I added my ornery neighbor to the list. Richie actually started to laugh.

"C'mon, Maggie, that guy's like 70. He's too old to be a murderer," Richie argued.

"One time my grandmother was watching *Columbo*, and the murderer was an old woman, and no one suspected her because she was so old, but she was poisoning people," I countered him.

"Okay, but we investigate him last. Mr. 'Feeble' couldn't kill a mosquito," Richie laughed.

We sat and thought for a minute, finishing our soggy fries.

"Listen, tomorrow is Gina's funeral. Meet me at Saint Christopher's at 10 am, and we can investigate Father Anthony after the Mass," I advised Richie, wanting to get started as soon as possible.

"Am I allowed in your church?" Richie asked, and I stared at him awkwardly, trying to think of an acceptable answer.

"Not because I'm Black, silly. Because I'm Baptist," he laughed at my reaction.

"Oh, of course. Yes, everyone can go, especially since it's a funeral; it's fine," I reassured him.

With our plans finalized, we walked back to the pools.

When we got back to Monica, she was packing up her bag. I realized then how hard it was for her to be anywhere in public right now. She was sitting alone, and no one was coming anywhere near her.

She eyed us suspiciously with a smile. "You two up to something?" she asked.

"Nope, just eating soggy French fries," Richie explained and winked at me.

"See you guys later," I said with a smile and a wave, and walked back to my sister.

My sister was deep in conversation with a girl from her class, Cynthia, when I got back to my towel. Cynthia had long, blonde hair and a big butt. I knew my sister didn't actually like Cynthia. She had once said she was "easy," but high school girl code meant you were nice to someone's face even if you said horrible things about them behind their back.

I sat on the towel and watched the faux friendly conversation unfold. I noticed that Cynthia was wearing a necklace. It was a necklace with her name on it, exactly like the one Gina had.

"Hey, Cynthia, where did you get that necklace?" I asked. She looked down at me as if it was absurd that I was there, let alone that I would speak to her.

"From a secret admirer," she grinned like the Cheshire Cat and turned her back to me to finish her conversation with my sister.

I took another look around the pool. Could the killer be there? Beyond the fence, I saw a familiar car in the parking lot, Ray's Red Trans Am. I scanned the pool and saw him. He was sitting across the pool from us, alone on the concrete. He was wearing cutoffs, sunglasses, and smoking a cigarette. But I felt like he was staring right at us. When Cynthia whipped around and pranced away, his head turned to follow her. I felt a shudder in my spine.

"God. Cynthia's an ass." Patty sat up and looked at me. "We leave in about a half-hour, Mags."

Then she flopped over to tan her back.

We rode our bikes home in the late afternoon, and I could tell by the awkward way Patty was riding her bike that she had a sunburn. She never learned. As we parked our bikes against the side of the house, I saw Mr. Feeney prowling around, looking at the parched bushes in his front yard.

I thought of Charlie, and all he was going through, and decided there was no time like the present to start my investigation. I took a deep breath, rallied myself, and walked over to him. I stood on his lawn for a minute, waiting for him to notice me, but he seemed oblivious.

"Hello, Mr. Feeney," I said as sunnily as possible. He turned in fright and his expression registered shock that I was standing there.

"What do you want?" he rasped at me.

"Well, I was just wondering if you needed any help with your yard?" I stammered out a reason for being there.

He appraised me skeptically and then responded.

"You looking to make money? Cause I don't pay kids for doing nothing," he hissed, and I noticed how ancient and shrunken he looked up-close. I was nearly as tall as he was.

"Just thought you might need some help," I continued. He stared into space for a long time.

"Mr. Feeney, do you need help with your yard?" I asked again, being sure to enunciate every word clearly. He flinched like I had hit him.

"Where I could use help is in the house. The lawn is fine," he stated, gesturing with his hand over his lawn, as if the patches of yellow grass were a great expanse of greenery.

"Follow me," he directed and marched toward the house. I followed nervously.

As the rusted screen door flapped behind us, I found myself standing in Mr. Feeney's living room, which had apparently not seen a cleaning or update since the Great Depression. Stacks of newspapers lined the walls, boxes of assorted sizes cluttered the floor with old dishes, Christmas ornaments, and rusted kitchen utensils. The air was musty, and just looking around at piles of randomness made me feel claustrophobic and hopeless all at once.

"So, you see, I've been organizing, but I think women are better at that," Mr. Feeney said with a chuckle, motioning to the clutter.

"Yeah, I guess, my mom does most of it," I answered vaguely.

He walked over to the dining room table, which was piled high with more boxes, and retrieved a small pad of paper and a pencil. Then he motioned for me to sit down. I sat at the chair farthest from him, wondering what I had gotten myself into.

"I will pay you a nickel an hour to help me organize," he stated and stared at me, evaluating my reaction. Then he scrawled something on the paper and passed it over to me. A nickel an hour? I guess it really was the Depression Era inside the Feeney house.

I looked at the paper and found a scribbled contract of sorts with a line for my signature. I stared at it for a moment.

"You know, Mr. Feeney, I will have to discuss this with my parents," I explained slowly, and he nodded in agreement.

"But I was wondering if you had seen Gina recently?" I asked with trepidation. He looked at me confused.

"Who?" he hooted and held his hand to his ear, which I noticed was sprouting more than a little bit of gray hair. I winced.

"Gina, my babysitter, have you seen her lately? Long brown hair, pretty," I repeated loudly.

He seemed to search his mind but was coming up empty.

"The hippie girl," I offered. "Gina," I said her name again, amplifying my voice.

"No, haven't seen her in years," he answered flatly.

"But she was on the street just this week. She babysits for the Johnsons," I reminded him.

"The who?" He craned his head, so his ear was closer to me.

"The Johnsons, the family with the baby," I explained.

"Never heard of 'em," he answered again abruptly, staring at me as if I was the crazy one.

I noticed a picture of his son Billy sitting on a bookshelf near the table. Mr. Feeney followed my glance and looked at the picture too. He pushed himself up from the table with a grunt, took the picture down, and handed it to me.

"That's my Billy. Handsome kid." He pointed at the picture and smiled sadly. His eyes were cloudy.

"He was, Mr. Feeney," I agreed. Billy had been really cute, and I had a hazy memory of Billy standing on the front porch of the Feeney's house in his Army uniform when I was around 4 or 5, back when Mrs. Feeney was alive. The whole neighborhood had gone over to wish him well before he shipped off to Vietnam. Six months later, two Army officials arrived at the Feeney house; Billy was dead. Mrs. Feeney died of cancer two years later.

I saw tears forming in Mr. Feeney's eyes, and I suddenly realized that the only thing scarier than Mr. Feeney angry was Mr. Feeney crying. I had no idea what to do.

"I'm sorry, Mr. Feeney," I mumbled and handed him back the picture.

"No matter," he said quietly, and gently placed the picture back on the shelf. He took a yellowed handkerchief out of his pocket and blew his nose violently, honking like a wild goose. Then he turned and looked at me, seeming startled to see me there. He looked around as if I had just appeared out of thin air.

"So, what do you want? Oh, the cookies!" he said and headed down the hallway of his house mysteriously. I had no idea what was happening.

While he was rummaging for whatever he was rummaging for, I decided to look around the house a bit more. A wedding picture of a young and happy Mr. and Mrs. Feeney was framed on the wall of the living room. I looked at it, shaken a bit by the fact that this smiling young man in the photo was now the stooped over, forgetful old man down the hall.

I snuck a peek in the kitchen. The sink was piled full of dirty dishes, and there were more stacks of magazines and newspapers in the kitchen. There was nothing in the house that seemed suspicious or nefarious. It was all just really dilapidated and depressing.

Mr. Feeney came walking back into the living room with a dollar bill, waving it at me.

"Is this what I owe you? For the cookies?" he asked, his head turned to the side as if he was trying to hear someone talking.

"No, you don't owe me anything," I said, edging towards the door.

"She paid you then," he said, and gestured towards the empty kitchen, as if his wife was in there doing dishes or cooking dinner, instead of years dead.

"Yes, sir," I said with a smile. He smiled back at me, and I noticed that he was missing one of his top front teeth.

"So, I'd better be going. I'll ask my parents about helping you organize," I said, waving his little contract in my hand.

"What? I don't need any help," he said gruffly, shooed me out the door, and slammed it behind me.

As I walked home, I realized I had eliminated one suspect. Mr. Feeney didn't know what year it was, he was pretty decrepit, and he didn't even remember Gina. I knew now why my mom had said he was tragic.

Later after dinner, I sat on our front steps and watched the little kids in my neighborhood running around with sparklers. Some of the girls from my school were at the end of the street, hanging out like a swarm of bees, buzzing around looking for activity. I knew better than to go near them; I'd just get stung again.

I saw Mr. and Mrs. Johnson on a blanket on their lawn with Baby Daisy, awaiting the town fireworks. We could see them from our neighborhood because the firehouse where they set them off was only two streets over. Even old Mr. Feeney was sitting in a dilapidated lawn chair, alone of course, watching the night sky. Whether he was looking for fireworks or German bombers was anyone's guess. Everything looked so normal, but it wasn't. I wondered if anything would ever feel normal again.

That night as I lay in bed, I could see more fireworks from my window, exploding colorfully in the sky. The brightness seemed vulgar to me now.

The world was so cruel. It kept spinning and celebrating even though Gina was gone.

I flashed on the image of Ray at the pool. Where was he on this fiery summer night? Gina said love made you crazy. Did that include the kind of crazy that could make someone commit murder? And did Ray love Gina like crazy?

Suspicious Minds

Wednesday, July 5, 1972

My mom told me I couldn't go to Gina's funeral. She claimed it would upset me, but I think she just didn't want to bring me and face it herself. I felt an obligation to be there for Gina. My mother was already mad at me, which made defying her seem easier. I decided to ride my bike to church.

I retrieved my balled-up graduation dress from the closet, smoothed it out, and put it on. I still didn't like how I looked in it, but Gina had liked it and that was what mattered. I tried to brush my hair into a neat ponytail, and I put on my best sandals. The dress was hot, and it wasn't the best outfit for bike-riding, but I wanted to look nice out of respect. As I pedaled, I tried to recall all my best memories of Gina. There were too many for such a short ride.

Even though Gina didn't attend Saint Christopher's School, and her mom and she weren't regular church-goers, Gina had been baptized there, so her funeral was being held at my church. When I arrived at Saint Christopher's, Richie was nervously waiting for me in the parking lot. He was wearing a white shirt and a tie with his jeans. I smiled when I saw him.

"Hey," I greeted him. "You look nice," I offered.

"You do too," he returned the compliment. We walked towards the church together in silence.

137

Before we got inside, I updated him about the necklace Cynthia had on at the pool, and the way Ray had stared at her.

"I wonder if he will be here," Richie speculated nervously.

"That would be so sick, if he was the one and then he went to her funeral," I asserted. The thought of seeing Ray in church made me anxious. But I needn't have worried; he wasn't there.

In fact, as we walked into the church, I was sad to see there were far fewer people in the church than I anticipated. Somehow, it no longer mattered that Gina had lived here her entire life and was kind to everyone. It only mattered that she was pregnant, and Charlie was presumed to be the father. Compassion for her had evaporated. I was shocked that the adults of my town would be so heartless, but as I had attended school with their children for the past seven years, I suppose I should not have been.

Richie sat next to me, trying his best not to fidget in the pew. I got the feeling the services he attended were considerably more energetic, even funerals. He copied my movements, standing, kneeling, and blessing himself awkwardly, and it struck me then what perfect manners he had.

Father Anthony was short in his eulogy, a generic message about God's love and salvation despite sin. What sin could he think Gina had committed? She was murdered. Father Anthony seemed afraid to compliment an unwed pregnant girl, even if she was a murder victim, which didn't say much for the mercy of the church or its parishioners. I was angry that Father Anthony didn't share one amazing Gina story when there were so many. It could have been a eulogy for anyone.

Throughout the funeral, I tried to avoid looking at the casket because I couldn't fathom how it could contain all the life and energy that was Gina. It was all so horribly surreal.

Gina's mom was in the front row, silently sobbing. I had met Gina's mom a few times, and she was very sweet. She had been a single mother forever, working as a waitress and struggling financially to take care of Gina. She had already suffered a hard life, and now her heart was permanently broken. Gina's dad had left when she was little, and as far as

I knew, no one ever heard from him. I wondered how he'd feel knowing he could never call his daughter now.

Richie said he saw a few Milford public school teachers in the pews in front of us, and I spied a couple of nuns from Saint Christopher's who attended every funeral in town, whether they knew the person or not. One nun had silent tears running down her cheeks, and I wondered if she cried for everyone, or if she knew Gina.

As the mourners headed to communion, I saw my father in line, and on the way back from communion, he saw me. I was shocked that he was there. Richie opted not to go to communion for fear of making a mistake and being identified as an imposter Catholic.

On the way out of church, my dad waited for me in the vestibule. He seemed surprised to see Richie with me. I looked up at him quizzically.

"Why are you here?" I asked.

"Same reason as you. To pay my respects. I have known Gina since she was a child. She was always a very sweet kid. She was good to you and your sister," he explained, and I teared up at his kindness. If we had been a different family, we could have attended Gina's funeral together. But in my family, everyone kind of existed in their own orbit. It was a lonely family.

"Hello, Mr. Murphy," Richie said politely.

"Hi, Richie, good to see you," my dad offered warmly.

"Don't tell mom I was here. She said no." I suddenly realized I was caught, disobeying her again.

"Your secret's safe with me, Maggie," he said and gave me a sad smile, and I realized she probably didn't know he was here either.

"Well, I have to get back to work. It's awfully hot. Do you two need a ride home?" he offered.

I didn't want my father to know about our investigation plans, so I made up an excuse.

"We'll ride our bikes. Don't want Mom to see us together and get us caught," I smiled at him.

"Good thinking," he smiled back and winked at us. And it felt nice to be conspiring with him.

Father Anthony was offering his condolences to the mourners as they were leaving, so I led Richie back to the offices of the church. Since the Church was attached to my elementary school, I knew exactly where Father Anthony's office was located.

We snuck into Father Anthony's unlocked office and looked around. It was sparsely furnished, but extremely tidy, with a large desk, one wilted plant, and a window that looked out onto the school playground. Books on the Bible and Catholic theology lined the walls of an oak bookcase. There were two frayed wingback chairs in rose velvet that I presumed were for private conversations with Father Anthony. I imagined that must have been where Gina sat when she spoke with him.

"Let's check his desk drawers," I whispered, and we hastily went through them, but there was nothing there but school stationery and more books. On his desk sat a picture of him with several boys from school on a camping trip and another of a woman I presumed was his mother.

There was no sign that Gina had been there or anything that would indicate he was a criminal of any kind. There really wasn't anywhere else to search, unless something was stashed in one of his many books.

"What are we looking for exactly?" asked Richie exasperated.

"That's the thing, we won't know till we find it," I said in frustration. Suddenly we heard voices outside in the hall, and the door swung open. Father Anthony looked extremely surprised to find the two of us in his office. Luckily, we were just standing there, no longer rifling through his personal possessions.

Father Anthony looked at us with concern. "Is everything okay here, Maggie?" he asked.

"Um, yes, this is my friend Richie, and we both loved Gina, and we had some questions," I stumbled to provide a reason for our presence in his office.

"Well, why don't you and Richie have a seat," he said, motioning to the two wingback chairs. He leaned against his desk and folded his arms, awaiting our questions. He still wore his purple funeral vestments, which made him look more intimidating.

"Well, when's the last time you saw Gina?" I asked. He looked at me confused, obviously anticipating questions of a more spiritual nature.

"I guess about a week ago," he spoke slowly, eyeing me with suspicion.

"Did she tell you anything?" I asked, trying to sound innocently curious. He shook his head at me.

"Maggie," he chastised me, "you know that anything Gina told me would be in complete confidence. I was her priest." He managed to make me feel ashamed, a Catholic talent.

"Sorry," I mumbled. "I just don't understand what happened."

"It's a tragedy, and I don't suppose we can understand. We need to put our faith in God," Father Anthony tried to console me.

"Well, did the police talk to you, so you could, like, help?" I tried to sound as casual as possible, but my voice was shaky.

"Maggie, those are matters for adults. The grown-ups will work this out. You shouldn't be worrying about these things," Father Anthony reminded me. He was trying to sound reassuring, but as with all things Catholic, it came out like a reprimand.

"Where do we go when we die?" Richie piped up. I suppose he thought if he kept Father Anthony talking, we might learn something of value.

"Well, that depends on how we live," Father Anthony explained. "I'm not sure what your faith is, Richie, but in the Catholic faith, good people go to heaven," he smiled broadly at Richie as he spoke, which I found odd and a bit startling. Up until that moment, I could not have said if Father Anthony even had teeth, and here he was revealing a gleaming smile.

I had always been invisible to Father Anthony. My only experience with him was watching him lurk ghoulishly in the shadows of the sacristy.

This was a whole different Father Anthony. He lit up for Richie. He had known Richie for five minutes, and he had known me for over a year, and he already liked Richie better. So typical.

"Yeah, I'm Baptist, that's what we believe too. It's very interesting," Richie nodded like he was fascinated, and I just stared at him. This wasn't getting us anywhere.

"Then Gina went to heaven?" I pressed Father Anthony for any information I could get. He scrutinized my face, trying to ascertain my motive.

"I would certainly hope so," he answered vaguely. It was getting hot in his office, and I wanted to leave. I stood up and pulled Richie up with me.

"Well, that's about it. Thanks, Father," I said with a big, fake smile.

"Richie, I presume you attend Milford Public?" Father Anthony asked earnestly.

"Yeah, I do," Richie answered plainly.

"Well, you know we have scholarship programs at Saint Christopher's that could help you attend here," Father Anthony said with his biggest smile.

"Nah, I'm good," Richie said quickly.

"Fair enough, but you know, Richie, anytime you want to discuss issues of faith, my door is always open. God loves Baptists, too," Father Anthony reassured Richie with a warm smile and shook his hand, clasping his other hand over Richie's arm. It was like a death grip. Then as an afterthought, he added, "You, too, Maggie. You know that."

With that, we scurried out the door and practically ran to our bikes.

"Okay, no offense, Mags, but that priest is one weird dude," he blurted out, eyes wide. "But I don't know if he's a murderer. He didn't seem to care about Gina either way," he observed.

"I don't know. He was vague, wouldn't tell us anything about her, and he was counseling her," I argued.

"Maybe we could investigate the rest of the suspects and see what we find out before we spend any more time on Father Freaky," Richie suggested.

"Okay, sounds good. Where do we start?" I asked him, feeling a bit deflated that our first foray in the investigation had yielded such scanty results.

Richie shrugged. This was my idea, after all. A thought occurred to me.

"You know, my uncle is at work right now. I guess I could go over to my grandma's and try to get in his room," I proposed.

"Do you need me to come with you?" Richie offered generously. I hesitated.

"My grandma is kind of a witch, and she says colored," I confessed with shame. Richie started to laugh.

"Geez, Maggie, do you think I never heard that before, especially from an old person?" he howled.

"It's embarrassing," I added sheepishly.

"It's not your fault. It'll be fine. Besides, you know I can charm her," he smiled with his dimples, and I laughed at his cockiness.

A House with Secrets

Richie followed me through the twists and turns of the city streets until we arrived at the dreary little two-family house where Grandma lived. Her house was always a thousand degrees in summer, and I dreaded the stifling air inside. We dumped our bikes on her lawn and scampered up the front steps.

I was a little afraid my grandma would drop dead of shock or a heart attack when we got there. I never visited her without my parents, and no one in my family ever visited anyone unannounced. But I thought the power of surprise might throw her off her game long enough for me to sneak into Uncle Jimmy's room. I took a deep breath and rang the doorbell. Richie peered in through the screen door looking for my grandma. There was no movement inside the house.

"Maybe she's not home. Maybe she's out with friends," he conjectured, as his grandma often visited with friends, attended Bible study, volunteered at church.

"No, she's always home. She doesn't have friends. Trust me, Edna's not that likable," I sneered, enjoying the small rebellion of using Grandma's proper name, thinking of all the times Grandma had criticized or pitied me.

After a few minutes, I rang the bell again, and Grandma materialized from the back of the house. She immediately looked alarmed seeing me on her doorstep.

"Maggie, what's wrong?" she cried, but didn't open the door to let us in. She was wearing one of those snap front floral housecoats, and her hand went to her head as if her hair was a mess. It wasn't. It was frozen in place as usual, a blue, cotton-candy halo hovering over her head. It was time for me to start acting. I forced a smile.

"Well, we were in the area, and I thought we should visit you," I offered as sunnily as possible, and Richie nodded his head furiously in agreement.

My mother had gotten her suspicious gene from my grandmother, so Grandma's eyebrows furrowed as she assessed us. She paused for a moment, but seemed unable to think of a nefarious reason for us to be there. Reluctantly, she opened the screen door and let us in.

"Well, I wasn't expecting anyone, so I am at a loss here," she sputtered at us as we walked in.

"Oh, we won't stay long, just saying hello," Richie reassured her and smiled, plopping down on her sofa. I giggled a little because in Grandma's house, it was customary to be asked to sit before one actually sat.

"You know, Grandma, it's hot out there," I said, and boiling in here I thought. "Could we have some water or something?" I asked politely.

"Oh my, I don't know what I have that you people would like. There's grapefruit and prune juice," she said reluctantly. Grandma's diet consisted mostly of things that would "help her system move." Richie made a face at the gross sound of those drinks.

"Just water would be great," I piped up, my voice full of the gratitude necessary to get her moving.

"Okay, well, you two sit here, and I'll get something," she answered, seemingly overwhelmed at having to bring two glasses of water from the kitchen to the living room.

As soon as she was out of sight, I shot up the backstairs.

I had to brace myself to enter the dreaded upstairs at Grandma's house. I ran past the bathroom and saw the door to Uncle Jimmy's bedroom, shut tight. He was pretty much the only one who ever went

145

upstairs because Grandma slept in the back bedroom downstairs. I found it curious and more than a little suspicious that he kept his door shut in the burning furnace of the second floor. I gently opened the door. I knew he would be at work, but I was nervous anyway.

Uncle Jimmy's room wasn't messy as I assumed it would be. It was tragically empty considering the fact that Uncle Jimmy had lived there his entire life. There was only a dresser, an end table, and an old bed with a quilt Grandma had sewn. But the bed was made, and the room seemed orderly.

I looked in the closet first. Behind Uncle Jimmy's janitor uniforms and boots, there were four huge stacks of dirty magazines on the floor. Naked women with glossy lips in vulgar poses. My stomach turned. On the shelf were spare blankets and a small Kodak camera. But other than the magazines, there was nothing unusual in his closet.

Next, I looked under the bed, but there was nothing there but a healthy crop of dust bunnies. I began to rifle through the dresser, and it was pretty revolting going through Uncle Jimmy's briefs. For my own sense of sanity, I told myself everything in the dresser was clean. Nothing but clothes in the dresser. The only thing left was the end table next to the bed. There was a Bible on it, which I am sure Grandma put there. I opened it. The binding was tight, and the wispy pages were stuck together, as if no one had ever read it.

I opened the end table drawer, and there was a cigar box inside. I placed it on the bed and opened it. Inside was a stack of photos of girls, high school girls. They weren't undressed or anything, but it was still creepy because you could tell the girls didn't know their pictures were being taken. They were just walking down the hall or eating in the cafeteria.

Underneath the photos were yearbook pictures of about a dozen girls that had been cut out and saved. I sifted through them and found Gina's. I felt my heart jump and my stomach lurch. Then I found a photo taken of Gina and Ray sitting in the school library. They were holding hands, and

Gina was smiling. This was evidence. I grabbed the pictures of Gina, and put the rest back in the box, placing the box back in the drawer.

I shut Uncle Jimmy's bedroom door behind me, dashed into the bathroom, flushed the toilet, and ran back downstairs.

Grandma and Richie were sitting in the living room, drinking water. There was a plate of saltines, stale I'm sure, sitting on the coffee table. What was it with my family and saltines? Did anyone on earth consider them a good snack?

"Sorry about that. Had to use the bathroom," I explained, aware I was sweating profusely. I had my hands behind my back, hiding the photos.

"Why didn't you use the downstairs, Maggie?" Grandma probed.

"I didn't want anyone to hear the toilet flush. You know, cause it's rude," I lied, trying to appeal to her sense of propriety. Her eyes opened wide, as if this had never occurred to her before, as if she had spent decades committing a horrific social faux pas without knowing it.

"Well, we'd better get going before our parents are wondering where we are," I announced suddenly, and Richie practically leapt from the sofa.

Grandma seemed to breathe a sigh of relief that this highly irregular and uncomfortable visit was over.

As we scooted out the door, I thought about covering our tracks.

"Grandma, maybe you shouldn't tell my parents I was here because I'm not supposed to ride my bike this far," I offered innocently.

Grandma seemed conflicted by the thought of keeping this secret, so I whispered gravely, "It might start a fight between my parents."

I knew that would seal her silence, as she was always worried my parents' fighting would lead to a divorce, an unspeakable humiliation for Grandma. She nodded her agreement.

As we got on our bikes, she called after us, "Thank you for coming by," but it sounded more like a question than a statement.

I shoved the photos into the basket of my bike. Then Richie and I began to pedal away, and he turned to me. "Man, Maggie, your family," he said with awe and shook his head.

"You don't know the worst of it," I replied and stopped as we turned the corner off Grandma's street. Richie stopped, too. I took the photos out of the bike basket and held them out for him to see.

"I found these in Uncle Jimmy's room," I said with shame. "And lots more of other girls. He's a pervert for sure," I said angrily.

"Wow, that is so freaky!" Richie stared, his mouth agape at the evidence I had found.

"I think we should bring these to the police. I think Uncle Jimmy did it!" I hissed angrily. Richie thought for a minute.

"It's definitely gross, but I'm not sure it's enough. They saw Charlie with Gina, and he's Black, and your uncle is white," Richie said with a heavy sigh.

"But he works at the high school. He knew her! And the pictures!" I waved the pictures in front of his face. I was more than a little unnerved by all the discoveries in Uncle Jimmy's room, given what I knew about my grandfather.

"We need something more if we want the police to listen to us," Richie insisted.

"What else could there be?" I asked desperately. Richie was quiet for a minute.

"Well, do you know if your uncle was home last Thursday?" Richie asked, and it occurred to me that was an excellent question.

"No, but I bet I can find out," I shot back, ready to take aim at Uncle Jimmy's fat ass. I guess the wild look in my eyes alarmed Richie because he put his hand on my arm to calm me.

"Maggie, we need to think about this before we do anything," Richie spoke softly and steadily.

"Okay, but I feel weird going home knowing that my uncle is such a pervert. What if he kills someone else before tomorrow?" I said, my voice quivering in fear.

"Listen, Maggie, if you bring that to the police, your mother will never speak to you again. And it's probably not enough to prove anything," he pointed out.

I sighed. He was right. The police seemed so sure it was Charlie. The local newspaper had all but convicted him. Even though Uncle Jimmy's pictures were sickening, they might not be enough to make the police budge. We needed more. And once I went to the police, I would pretty much be an orphan. My mother would never forgive me.

"Maybe we can find more evidence if we go there?" Richie said suddenly.

"Huh?" I asked.

"To Pirate's Island. Maybe there's evidence. The police probably didn't even look because they just focused on Charlie," he offered. "Maybe there will be something there to tie your uncle to Gina," he explained.

"That's a good idea. Something else combined with the pictures," I got excited at the thought of really nailing Uncle Jimmy.

"And if we are going to the police to say it's your uncle, we have to be sure. We don't want to blow our chance because then the police will never listen to us again," he reminded me gravely.

I nodded, trying to absorb the reality of the situation. I felt sure Uncle Jimmy was guilty, but I agreed that more evidence was better.

"Okay, but we have to go to Pirate's Island when it's dark. The area is still roped off with police tape, and there are teams practicing in those fields all day with coaches and stuff. I rode by yesterday. No one can see us go in there," I explained.

Richie stopped and looked at me, trying to figure out if I was serious. He was usually the one willing to take a chance. But ever since I had exploded at my parents, I felt brave and I liked it.

"I mean it. I'm not afraid. Okay, I am kind of afraid, but I still want to do it," I insisted. He paused in thought so long, I worried I had upset him.

"But our parents aren't letting us out after dark," he reasoned.

"So, we sneak out. I can sneak out after my parents fall asleep. I'll ride my bike over. How about midnight?" I felt bold and scared all at once. We stared at each other for a minute.

"Come to my window and I'll sneak out too," he agreed, nodding, and we shook on it.

"Bring a flashlight," I added.

I couldn't believe we were actually going to do this, but for the first time since Gina had died, I didn't feel powerless.

"Okay, well I'd better get home now. If my parents figure out that I'm not in my room, they'll have a fit. They were upset this morning about some newspaper article that they said made Charlie sound like a crazy killer. They are afraid for me to be anywhere but home," he explained.

I felt so ashamed of my town again. Why should Richie's parents have to worry about him too?

We parted halfway between our houses, but instead of a smiling goodbye, we just waved and stared at each other for a minute, knowing we would next meet at midnight to visit the scene of a murder.

When I finally arrived on my street, my stomach flipped when I saw my house. When I first suggested Uncle Jimmy as a suspect, I had been theorizing, caught up in the fantasy of me as a detective. But now I had pictures that proved my own family member was potentially a murderer. I parked my bike on the far side of the house away from my parents' window, and I walked slowly up the front steps, dreading going inside and facing my family.

Under a Moonless Sky

At dinner that night, over burnt lasagna, I tried to do a little detective work. Now that I was on this road, there was no going back.

"So, Mom, has Uncle Jimmy ever had a girlfriend?" I asked innocently. Patty spit out her milk in laughter. My mother gave her a glare, but she was too distracted by the fact that I was speaking to her again to reprimand Patty. Instead, she answered me politely.

"Uncle Jimmy is very devoted to taking care of Grandma, you know that," my mother explained, as if I was a kindergartener and would buy that line.

"Uncle Jimmy doesn't have a girlfriend because he's a whale and a janitor," Patty jeered and laughed like a hyena. I waited for my mother to slap her.

"Patricia, I will not have you insulting your uncle! He works extremely hard, and he is the head of maintenance for the high school, a very responsible job," she defended her brother stridently. I caught my dad rolling his eyes.

"Sorry," Patty mumbled insincerely. My mother seemed a bit mollified.

"Do you know what he does on, say, Thursday nights?" I asked casually. All three of my family members were staring at me trying to understand my newfound interest in Uncle Jimmy's social life.

"He bowls every Thursday. In fact, last week, he came in first for the league," my mother beamed as if her brother had been awarded the Nobel Prize. My dad rolled his eyes again. I was glad she didn't see him. That would have caused a major explosion.

"Grandma said when he got home on Thursday, he was so happy," she smiled as if Jimmy was a little kid.

"And then he didn't leave again?" I asked, trying to sound casual.

"Maggie, what are you getting at?" my mother eyed me shrewdly, and I knew I had pushed too far.

"Nothing. It's just I don't really know Uncle Jimmy well, and he's my uncle," I offered weakly.

"Well, that's ridiculous. You've known him your entire life," she answered irritably.

She got up and started furiously scrubbing dishes and jamming them in the dishwasher. The rest of us continued to eat in silence. When she was finished, she slammed the dishwasher shut.

"I swear, Maggie, you are just the strangest child." She glared at me and left the kitchen, the door flapping behind her. Considering the other insults she had hurled at me over the years, strange was mild.

After she was out of earshot, Patty sneered, "Uncle Jimmy's the strange one. Freaking weirdo." She had no idea how correct she was, and I wished I could tell her, but I knew she would immediately run to my parents with the pictures. That would give my mother a chance to tip off Uncle Jimmy, and I couldn't let that happen. If Uncle Jimmy did murder Gina, I wasn't going to let him get away with it.

My father, Patty, and I loaded our plates into the dishwasher and left the kitchen without saying another word.

After dinner, I watched a little TV and then said goodnight around 9:30 to both of my parents, who were reading in the living room. I sat at my desk and read *The Wizard of Earthsea* by flashlight. I had to turn out my light, or Patty might see it and wonder why I was still awake. She was nosy that way, and she had a keen instinct for any kind of trouble. At 10:00, she turned her light off.

I was too wired to read anymore, but it was still too early to leave, so I started to doodle on my desk blotter. I drew animals, cars, houses, anything to occupy my mind. My Trix Rabbit sticker glowed in the dark, and I felt a chill looking at it.

By 11:30, I figured my parents, both early risers, would be deep asleep. They slept with a large fan in their bedroom, and I was counting on the white noise to cover any sounds I might make.

I crept like an alley cat down the stairs. I went out the back door, making sure to shut the screen door, which normally slammed, as gently as possible. I tiptoed to the side of the house opposite my parents' bedroom, where I had left my bike. I was relieved my mother hadn't noticed it missing from its usual spot.

I pedaled in the dark, streetlights guiding my way. I rode fast, propelled by fear and excitement. I was sure we would find something to lead us to the real killer. The moon was missing from the sky, obscured by clouds, making the night darker and eerier than I thought possible.

I arrived at Richie's house and threw a small pebble at his window. Almost immediately, his head popped up and he opened the window. He shimmied out the window with ease, a benefit of being skinny and agile. He dropped to the ground and ran for his bike. We looked at each other in silence and pedaled toward the school.

I followed him, getting only glimpses of him in staccato punches under streetlights.

We passed the school parking lot and arrived at the path that led to the sports fields. We rode down the path closest to Pirate's Island. We plopped our bikes by the edge of the grass and walked the rest of the way. Once we arrived at Pirate's Island, we stood together for a minute, staring at the dark thicket of trees. On one side of Pirate's Island were wild raspberry bushes, and I flashed back to a day three summers earlier when Gina, Patty, and I went raspberry picking. We ate so many as we picked the branches bare that we had hardly any to bring home for my mother to make pie or jam.

We considered telling our mother that there weren't many raspberries to pick, but Gina pointed out our faces would give us away. We had Joker smiles from the raspberry stains. We started laughing and couldn't stop all the way home. Our bellies hurt from too many raspberries and laughter. Standing here in the dark, that day seemed more like a dream than a memory. The area seemed ominous now, and the trees looked much larger and denser in the dark.

Richie turned on his flashlight and headed in first, ducking under the yellow police tape. I wondered briefly if we could be arrested for what we were doing, but then figured it was too late to worry about that now. I caught up to him and turned on my flashlight. We walked for a bit in silence, but all we saw were trees and dirt and leaves. Occasionally, a toad would croak, or a bird would squawk, and we would both freeze suddenly.

Eventually my flashlight hit upon a smaller area of yellow tape strung up by a big rock. I felt lightheaded, confronted by the reality of being there. It seemed both haunted and holy. As we walked closer, I could see a depression in the grass where her body must have been. Gina had lain here dead, waiting for someone to find her. I felt myself start to cry. Richie sat down outside the perimeter of the depression. He motioned for me to sit. I did.

"What are we looking for?" he asked, whispering even though no one could hear us.

"Anything," I said. "Do you see anything here?" He flashed the light around the area. I tried to imagine who could have taken Gina here.

We examined the area with my flashlight, looking for anything the killer might have left behind. Richie was kicking at the dirt to see if anything was concealed, and I was examining the rock for any evidence. I found a cigarette butt.

"Look!" I hissed, holding it up.

"Does your uncle smoke?" Richie asked excitedly.

"No, but Ray does, all the time," I told him, and he nodded solemnly.

"Maybe the police could prove whose cigarette this is, by the brand, and that might be the killer," Richie suggested, so I put the cigarette butt in a plastic baggy I had brought along for evidence.

We continued to examine the area for anything that might link Uncle Jimmy to the crime. But all we could find were leaves and dirt. There didn't seem to be any evidence to discover. Richie was poking leaves around with a stick he found, but whatever we were hoping to find just wasn't there.

"I asked my mom about Uncle Jimmy at dinner. She said he was bowling Thursday night, and won some contest, and then he went home. But that doesn't mean he didn't go back out," I shared my latest information. My heart was as heavy as it had ever been.

"We need to think, Maggie. C'mon," Richie said, and he took my hand and led me to the rock, where we sat and discussed our suspects again. Uncle Jimmy was number one in my book.

"We don't know about Father Anthony. I guess Ray is still a suspect, but I think Uncle Jimmy is the one," I said heavily.

"You left off Mr. 'Feeble,'" Richie said, reminding me of my initial list.

"Yeah, he's off the list. I talked to him yesterday, or at least, I tried to. He doesn't even know what year it is," I explained with a sigh.

"Yeah, I told you. He's too old," Richie reasoned. "Gina could've fought him off," he concluded.

"True, but if the person had a weapon, they don't have to be strong," I offered.

"She was strangled, Maggie," he said hesitantly. I hadn't known how she had been killed, didn't want to think about it, and I felt like someone had punched my chest.

"Sorry, Maggie." Richie squeezed my hand.

"It's okay," I lied, but suddenly I felt a million times worse and more than a little terrified to be out in the dark in the middle of an area hidden by trees.

"I heard my parents talking. The cops kept saying how strong Charlie is…" his voice trailed off and he put his head down.

"It doesn't matter. They are wrong. We will prove it," I reassured him.

We sat in heavy silence, trying to think of anything that could help us.

"Maybe we should say a prayer," Richie said quietly.

I squeezed his hand in agreement.

"Gina, please help us find who did this to you," Richie began speaking in a solemn voice. "Then you can rest in peace, and Charlie can be free," he finished.

"Let's say the "Our Father" together," I suggested, so in whispered voices, we prayed.

"Our Father who art in heaven…deliver us from evil. Amen."

Evil. I could almost feel it in the dark night air.

We sat in silence for a moment and looked around at the murky woods. I wondered why we thought it was a good idea to come here, especially at midnight.

All of a sudden, I saw a shadow in the distance. Some leaves crunched. I froze.

"Richie," I whispered in a panic, "I think there's someone over there."

He looked up, and the shadow moved again. In unison, we hunched down, huddling together.

"I think we should leave. There's nothing here. No clues," I murmured. Then we heard the sound of someone walking toward us.

We both turned and ran, stumbling over uneven dirt and pushing through tree branches. Richie exploded into the clearing first, and I followed. As we were climbing on our bikes, I saw a man running out of Pirate's Island on the side. He began sprinting toward us at what seemed to be superhuman speed. It was Ray.

"Hey, Maggie, wait up," Ray yelled. Even in the dark, I could see the frenzied look on his face. My heart was pounding.

"Go!" I yelled, and we pedaled as fast as we could. Ray continued to follow us, but he gave up by the time we reached the school parking lot. I turned back to see him leaning over, hands on knees, panting. I was glad he was a heavy smoker.

We rode just as fast all the way home. When we arrived at Richie's house, we just stared at each other wordless, unsure what anything meant. I made a step with my hands, and Richie climbed back into his window. I flew home and snuck back in bed. I tucked the baggy with the cigarette in my journal, with the pictures from Uncle Jimmy's drawer.

I was still shaking when I fell asleep.

It Just Gets Murkier

Thursday, July 6, 1972

Richie called me in the morning, and I dragged the kitchen phone cord into the hall for privacy. We were both pretty shaken up after the night before, wondering if Ray had been following us and why.

"What should we do next?" Richie asked me, breathless. What had started as some simple attempts to get information had turned into a dangerous endeavor.

"I don't know. I was so sure it was Uncle Jimmy, but why was Ray there? Why did he chase us?" I wondered aloud.

"Maybe it is Ray after all," Richie suggested. But I still didn't think so.

"But she was pregnant. Why would Ray hurt his own baby?" I said, feeling my stomach hurl at the mere thought of what Gina had suffered.

"Because she dumped him, and he was angry," he reasoned, and then added in a whisper, "Or maybe he didn't want a baby."

"Wow, that would be so evil," I was stunned at the thought. But I found it too hard to believe.

"I just don't know. I still think it's Uncle Jimmy," I argued. We paused and thought for a moment.

"What about the other girl you saw at the pool? The one Ray was watching," Richie asked.

"Cynthia? What about her? Why does she matter?" I asked.

"Well, you said she told you a secret admirer gave her the necklace," he reminded me.

"So, that could've been anyone," I sputtered, frustrated by what seemed irrelevant information.

"Well, if Ray gave her the necklace, and he is dating her now, she could know something important. Maybe Ray murdered Gina to be with her," he conjectured.

"You haven't met Cynthia. That would be really hard to imagine," I spouted sarcastically. "And I don't know if he's dating her, just that he was watching her," I added, getting more confused.

"Well, maybe if we can prove Ray bought those necklaces, then we will know he has some relationship with her," he offered.

"And then what?" I asked him, not seeing how this would get us anywhere.

"Well, we tell her how we saw him on Pirate's Island and ask for her help. She could be in danger," Richie said nervously.

"So, what do we do next?" I asked him, perplexed by so much confusing and conflicting information.

"We go to the jewelry store and find out who bought the necklaces," he declared firmly.

"And if we can find out who bought the necklaces, what then?" I asked, still uncomfortable with what I knew about Uncle Jimmy and waiting any longer. My gut was telling me he was guilty of something.

"Well, if it is Ray, we talk to what's-her-name," he offered hopefully.

"It's Cynthia," I reminded him. But I wasn't sold on the plan. "You don't think we should go to the police with the stuff I found in Uncle Jimmy's room?" I asked nervously.

"Let's just do this first, and maybe we will know more, and if we don't, then we'll go to the police," Richie laid out a plan.

"I guess. I don't know," I was wavering, feeling guilty and scared all at once.

"Listen, Mags, no one wants to help Charlie more than I do. This is ruining my family. But I don't want your family messed up if we are wrong. We do this one last thing and see if we can get answers," he argued. I thought for a minute and relented.

"Okay, I'll be over around one," I agreed.

I ran upstairs and hastily put on an old t-shirt and some gym shorts that were castoffs of Patty's. I put my crazy hair in a ponytail. I ran back down the stairs.

I made a sloppy PB&J and grabbed a handful of Cheese Jax. I knew my mother wouldn't approve of my lunch or of me eating out of the bag, but she was outside in her garden. I ate fast and drank a glass of water standing at the kitchen sink, watching my mother gently make beds of dirt around her flowers.

I had to tell her something to leave the house. I wiped my face with a paper towel, smoothed my hair, and went out the back screen door. I stood on the porch and yelled to her.

"Hey, Mom, I'm going to jump rope down the street. With girls," I lied.

She looked up at me, kneeling by her bed of lilies, her eyes squinting in the sun, and just nodded.

We both knew I was lying, and I realized how easily I lied to her these days. But more than that, I realized how little she seemed to care. We were mostly avoiding each other since our big fight, and I wondered if our relationship would ever feel normal.

Outside I saw Mrs. Johnson with baby Daisy on the front lawn. Daisy was taking a few hesitant steps toward her mother's outstretched arms, and I thought what a beautiful picture it would make. I was suddenly struck with fear at the thought of how vulnerable Daisy was in this dangerous world. I wanted to run over to Mrs. Johnson and tell her to never let Daisy out of her sight, but I knew how crazy I would sound. I got on my bike and pedaled as fast as I could, more determined than ever to identify the killer and get him locked up.

Richie and I rode to Fletcher's Jewelers, a small, family-owned place in the little retail strip in our town, next to a coffee shop and a card shop. People called the area "downtown," which was a joke considering the entire area was only about ten stores and the bus station.

Fletcher's looked to be on its last breath of life, carpet ratty and worn, dirty windows that looked as if they hadn't been washed in a decade, dead flies on the sills. Mr. Fletcher was an old man with thick glasses. He wore a yellowed, short-sleeved dress shirt and a tie that only reached the middle of his stomach; he barely noticed when we walked in.

Richie and I looked around for a minute at the rings and necklaces packed in three glass cases. I was anxious for answers, so I decided to just ask the old man for help.

"Hey," I offered with a smile that I hoped could distract from my scrappy appearance. "Do you sell those necklaces with girls' names on them?" I asked.

He appraised me for a minute, then motioned to a spinning necklace display on the counter near the register, and I saw all the names on it. I even saw "Margaret" and it gave me a queasy feeling. Richie started spinning them around. It seemed like every name in the universe was there.

"Do you sell lots of these?" I asked. The old man took off his glasses and stared at me. His breath smelled like stale coffee.

"What do you kids want? I got mirrors, and I can see if you steal. I'll call the cops." He shook a crooked finger at me.

"I just want to know if a man has been buying these necklaces, like recently," I asked. He shrugged to express his disinterest in anything I had to say.

"Please," I begged. "It's really important to me. You see, I think my dad is cheating on my mom, and I need to know for sure," I implored him, not sure where that very vicious lie came from and praying he would never find out who I was.

Richie looked at me, shocked at my deceit. I made my most forlorn face and stared at the old man. He eyed me suspiciously.

161

"Look, I don't want any trouble. I'm sorry," he replied with palms up as if to indicate his inability to help me.

"But I need to know before I say anything to my mom. See, I think he's going to leave her, and we will be poor because my mom is sick and can't work," I continued to lie, painting as pathetic a picture as possible.

Mr. Fletcher sighed deeply.

"Please help me save my family," I implored, laying it on thick. Old Fletcher stared at the ceiling, exasperated.

"There's been a guy who has bought a few," he offered vaguely.

"How many?" I shot back. He paused for a moment, seeming to decide if he was going to answer my question.

"Five or six, had to special order a couple, unusual names," he added cryptically.

Richie and I exchanged looks, and I felt a chill run down my spine.

"What's his name?" Richie popped up excitedly.

"He paid cash. I don't know his name," the old man answered flatly.

"Well, what did he look like?" I asked as politely as I could.

"Young guy, tall, scruffy. Too young to be your dad, I think," he offered as a reassurance.

"Oh, they had me when they were 13," I answered, and old Mr. Fletcher looked horrified.

"Was he handsome? Cause people say my dad looks like a movie star," I asked, trying to figure out if it could have been Ray after all. I couldn't deny that Ray was a good-looking guy.

"As handsome as a hippie can be," he sneered. I wished I'd had a picture of Ray to show the old dude.

"One more thing. Did he have long brown hair and wear a leather jacket," I asked.

The old man seemed to search his memory. "Not sure about the jacket, but definitely long brown hair."

"Anything else you remember?" I asked.

"He had a grin that was arrogant...like the cat that swallowed the canary," he shared.

"The what?" Richie asked, confused. But I shushed him.

"Anything else you remember? Did you see his car?" I prodded the old man for more information, but his patience for our questions evaporated. He began to eye us with some suspicion.

"Okay, time for you two to leave," Mr. Fletcher announced, swatting us away, and we headed for the door.

As an afterthought he shouted, "Sorry about your folks."

"Oh, yeah. Thanks. I'm sure they'll work it out," I shouted back. The old man stared at me like I was mad. Five or six mistresses didn't sound like a savable marriage.

Richie and I walked back outside to our bikes. We mounted them but sat there for a minute. It was a blisteringly hot July day.

"What do we do now?" he asked me. I tried to think.

"Well, the description of the guy who bought the necklaces does fit Ray," I answered.

"So, we need to talk to that girl," Richie reasoned.

"I don't know. Maybe the necklace has nothing to do with Gina's murder at all. I still think Uncle Jimmy is guilty. He had the pictures," I said angrily.

"Yes, your uncle is a creep and a perv, but that doesn't mean he murdered Gina. You said yourself he was with your grandmother Thursday night," he reminded me.

"What does she know? Housecoat lady," I sputtered in disgust.

"Maggie, you don't know it's your uncle. We saw Ray at the scene of the crime, we found the cigarette there, and he chased us!" Richie reminded me of our dangerous encounter with an angry Ray.

I paused my tirade against my family and listened to his reasoning.

"And now we have some evidence that he bought Gina and that other girl necklaces. And you said he was watching her at the pool," Richie was talking excitedly.

"Cynthia, the other girl is Cynthia, and she's an ass," I quoted my sister's succinct description. "But what difference does it make if he bought girls necklaces? He doesn't have sneaky, creepy pictures of Gina," I reminded him.

"Okay, so maybe Gina found out Ray was cheating on her with Cynthia," Richie continued and enunciated every syllable of Cynthia like it was a foreign language.

"I doubt that. You haven't seen Cynthia!" I sneered.

"Listen, maybe Ray and Gina fought about that, and she told him she was pregnant, and he got mad and snapped," Richie theorized, making a crazy face for emphasis. "Plus, Ray has more of a motive than your uncle does. Ray and Gina broke up, and we don't know why that happened. And you said yourself, he was looking for her the day she died, and he was angry," he finished.

"He did look crazy that day," I recalled the desperation and anger in Ray's eyes. I was so confused. I never thought we'd find two serious suspects.

"I'll ask my sister for Cynthia's phone number and see if she will meet with us," I said.

"But you need to make up a reason, not Ray. If she likes him, she'll cover for him," Richie argued.

"What possible reason would I have to talk with Cynthia?" I asked in exasperation.

"Patty, say you need to talk about Patty," Richie offered.

"That would work. Cynthia is a total gossip. If I ask for advice about Patty, she'll bite," I replied, thinking about how eager Cynthia would be to get dirt on my sister.

"Okay, that's the plan," Richie agreed.

"Then depending on what we find out, we bring our evidence for both suspects to the police," I suggested.

"Maybe. But I think the more sure we are, the better we can convince the police. Let's hope Cynthia knows something important," Richie stated firmly.

"No matter what she says, I'll write down our evidence for both suspects. They both know Gina. Uncle Jimmy talked about how pretty she was, and we have his pictures. Gina dumped Ray, and he was looking for her the day she died. Plus, we have what might be Ray's cigarette, and he chased us. I mean this has to at least give them a reason to investigate, right? And then they can stop blaming Charlie," I reassured Richie.

"Maybe you should be a lawyer, Maggie," he advised me with a smile.

"Maybe, but I still want to be a writer," I answered.

"You can be both. You can be anything. You're really smart," he encouraged me. I wish I had half the faith in myself that Richie had in me.

"So can you," I answered back.

"Yeah, but I am going to be a dancer and choreographer," he insisted and did a goofy wiggle on his bike.

"We are going to figure this out. We are going to get Charlie out of this," I promised him, and we fist-bumped like the Wonder Twins we were.

"Look, I have to get home before my grandma does. Get Cynthia's number and set up a meeting. We can talk on the phone later and plan it, and as soon as we have enough evidence, we go to the cops," he articulated a plan.

"Okay, sounds good," I agreed. By this time tomorrow, hopefully Charlie would no longer be the police's number one suspect.

"Call me after dinner," Richie called to me as he rode away, and I nodded my agreement and waved back.

As I rode my bike home, I was composing my letter of evidence in my head. With every block, I became more confused about whether Ray or Uncle Jimmy was the right suspect. Ray was furious with Gina for breaking up with him, and maybe he just lost it. That's why he was on Pirate's Island, to see what he left behind or something. Maybe he remembered he left the cigarette there. And he chased us because we knew the truth.

But Uncle Jimmy obviously had a weird fixation on Gina, and he was an old man taking pictures of young girls. Maybe he took his obsession too far. I felt so overwhelmed, I was panting. Between the heat and my fear, I was gasping for breaths.

Listening to Ghosts

When I finally arrived on my street, I pedaled slowly, the weight of the world on my shoulders. The street seemed eerily quiet for a summer afternoon.

Old Mr. Feeney was not on his front porch ready to yell at me when I rode by. Mrs. Johnson was no longer on her front lawn playing with Baby Daisy.

As I got closer to the Johnsons' house, I saw a woman come out the front door and stand for a minute talking to someone in the house. At first, I thought it was Mrs. Johnson, but long blonde hair and a big butt came into view, and I recognized Cynthia. I nearly fainted. This was my chance. It had to mean something. Maybe Gina was sending me the information I needed by giving me this chance encounter.

I crossed the street and paused by the Johnsons' house. Cynthia came bounding down the front steps, smiling. I noticed she was wearing a lot of makeup.

"Hey Cynthia." I got off my bike and approached her, determined to find out what she knew. She seemed surprised as if she had been too dazed to notice me there.

"Oh, Hey Maggie," she waved pleasantly at me. Again, I noticed her gold necklace. I could almost make out a shadow still standing behind the screen in the doorway of the Johnsons' house.

"Were you babysitting for the Johnsons?" I asked, and she seemed to blush.

"Well, I will be. I was just going over some stuff with Mr. Johnson about how much he will be paying me and hours and stuff," she smiled as she spoke. She acted as if it had never been Gina's job, as if Gina had never existed. I was angry.

But something was starting to make sense. Cynthia was with Ray, and now she had taken over Gina's babysitting job. It's like Cynthia was taking over Gina's life. Was Cynthia obsessed with Gina?

I noticed Mrs. Johnson's cute VW Bug was not in the driveway.

"Did you see the baby? Just now?" I asked. Cynthia's nose crinkled and she frowned at me.

"Not today," she answered curtly. She touched her necklace. Then she turned to leave, but I wasn't letting her get away that easily. I grabbed her arm. She spun around, surprise in her eyes.

"Who gave you that necklace?" I asked her boldly.

"Let go of my arm," she yelled, seeming terrified of me.

"The necklace. Did Ray give it to you?" I repeated, saying each word slowly for emphasis as if she was too stupid to understand, which I had decided she was.

"Who is Ray?" she stared at me as if I was insane, shaking her arm loose from my grip.

"Ray Bruno. Gina's ex. You know exactly who I'm talking about," I said angrily.

"What are you talking about? I have never said one word to that guy. He's a dirtbag," she huffed at me, as if she was far above the likes of Ray.

"Well, why was he staring at you at the town pool?" I shot back.

"What? How should I know? I don't know him. Like I said, he's a loser. He was Gina's boyfriend. She obviously had a deeply troubled life," Cynthia offered her unsolicited opinion on Gina.

Cynthia knew something—I was sure of it. And I didn't believe her dismissal of Ray. She could call him a dirtbag, but he was far better looking than anyone who would date her. I couldn't see her turning him down if he asked.

A curious thought occurred to me then.

"How did you even end up with Gina's job? How do you know the Johnsons? You go to Saint Christopher's and you don't live around here," I questioned her, feeling puzzle pieces form a picture in my brain.

She gave me a condescending smile. "It's really none of your business, Maggie. I mean I'm not really even friends with your sister, so I don't know why I'm even wasting my time talking to you," she shot back snarkily at me.

"I think you know something, Cynthia," I accused her.

"You know what? You're an impudent little brat," Cynthia snorted at me. And with that, she turned in a huff and walked toward her car parked in the street.

"Wait, I have more questions. Please, don't go," I pleaded with her, afraid my chance at finding out the truth was disappearing.

But Cynthia ignored me and got in her car, flipping me off as she drove away.

I stood frozen on the sidewalk, my brain swimming in too many thoughts, trying to unravel all the threads of information we had discovered. Did Cynthia really not know Ray? If not, why had he been staring at her? If not Ray, who gave her the necklace? Were they secretly having a relationship, as Richie guessed? Could Cynthia have something to do with Gina's murder?

I looked up at the Johnsons' house and was struck by the thought that Mr. Johnson might know something about Cynthia. I wasn't done here. Something came into focus, and a strange sense came over me that I wasn't alone. I could almost feel Gina standing next to me on the sidewalk.

A conviction deep inside propelled me forward. Before I knew it, I was on the front steps ringing the doorbell.

Mr. Johnson appeared out of the shadows, and he smiled at me.

"Hey Maggie, how are you?" he asked pleasantly.

"I'm okay. I saw Cynthia. Where are Mrs. Johnson and Daisy? I wanted to see the baby," I sputtered a reason for being there.

"They aren't here right now. Maybe another time," he smiled at me through the haze of the screen. His face became blurry in the shadows.

All of a sudden, I started to sway, and the next thing I knew, Mr. Johnson was helping me in the house and sitting me on the sofa. I sat there dazed, and he handed me a glass of lemonade. I must have fainted on the porch.

"Whoa, you gave me a scare, kiddo," he said. "You just went sideways on my porch! Have you had enough to drink today? It's hot. You might be dehydrated. Get your bearings, and I'll walk you home," he said with concern. I sat for a minute, until I could focus.

Their house looked just as I had imagined it. Cool funky colors, bean bag chairs, shag rug, and where our house had a swinging door into the kitchen, they had hung multi-colored beads. A mirror with an orange arrow painted on it hung on the wall across from the sofa. There was a huge stereo with enormous speakers, no television, and lots and lots of stacks of books.

"So, Cynthia is babysitting for you now?" I asked Mr. Johnson and gulped the glass of lemonade. He looked at me with curiosity and pushed his feathered hair back from his face.

"Looks that way," Mr. Johnson said pleasantly.

"She's replacing Gina?" I asked, although it wasn't really a question. His face showed concern.

"I'm sorry, Maggie. It must be hard for you to see someone replacing Gina in this job," he offered kindly.

"Yeah, it's weird."

"I know it's such a shock, and at your age, these things leave a lasting impression. I remember a young man in my graduation class who died the spring of our senior year. He was swimming at a local quarry, and he dove in and hit his head on a rock, died instantly. It was very bloody, I do remember that." Mr. Johnson spoke in a sad voice, as if the memory still pained him.

"That is sad. But at least he wasn't murdered," I said bluntly and then felt embarrassed by my candor.

"No, Gina's death is especially horrific, to say the least," he said softly.

"Do you know if Cynthia is dating Ray, Gina's ex?" I asked boldly. He appeared perplexed by my question.

"I don't really know much about Cynthia, other than that she comes highly recommended by other parents," Mr. Johnson replied, eyeing me curiously.

"What do you know about her? Because it just seems like she is kind of replacing Gina everywhere," I said sharply.

"Well, I'm sure it seems like that to you, but I assure you, Cynthia is just looking to make some money babysitting," he talked to me calmly as if I were unhinged.

"I'm not sure you can trust her. She's not a nice person," I warned him, leaning forward on the sofa.

"I heard they have a likely suspect in Gina's, um, death," Mr. Johnson offered, trying to change the subject.

"They have the wrong suspect," I said sharply, then regretted my tone.

"Maybe I should walk you home now," Mr. Johnson offered with a smile, keen to get me and my impertinent questions out of his house.

"Okay," I said, but as I stood up, I was hit with a wave of nausea.

"Where's your bathroom?" I jumped up and covered my mouth. He saw what was coming and ushered me down the hall to the bathroom.

As soon as I shut the bathroom door, I violently puked up the lemonade and my lunch of Cheese Jax and PB&J. Most of it went into the toilet, but a good amount splattered on the back of the toilet and the floor. My mother would be mortified to know I made such a mess in someone else's bathroom. I tried to wipe it up with toilet paper, but the toilet paper just disintegrated in my hand. I even managed to puke in the cat litter box next to the toilet.

I took a deep breath to calm myself. I needed to get a grip. I was acting crazy, desperate to figure out what happened to Gina. Suddenly, I wondered what I was doing here, making crazy claims about Cynthia to my handsome neighbor. Had I lost my mind? I felt dizzy again, and I was sweating. My emotions were out of control. I was confused and overwhelmed. Competing theories and thoughts were teeming in my head.

I would clean this mess up. Then I would go home and tell Patty what was going on. She could help me with Cynthia. Cynthia might not be a murderer, but she was hiding something. I was sure of it.

There were no towels in the bathroom, so I looked under the sink for anything I could use to clean. The only things I could find were a tub of cat litter and a big metal popcorn tin with one of those tops that were always impossible to pull off. I took it out and sat on the back of the toilet, using all my strength to yank the top free. It came off with a pop, and I hit my face with the back of my hand. Great, now I'd have a black eye too.

Luckily there were some old rags in the tin that I could use to sop up the mess. I figured no one would care if I used them, and when I finished cleaning, I would just hide them underneath some toilet paper in the wastebasket. Under the rags were some matchboxes, old batteries, and a dried-out sponge. I was about to put the lid back on when something shiny caught my eye. I reached my hand in the bottom of the tin, and I pulled the shiny object out. There in Mr. Johnson's bathroom, under the sink, in a metal tin, was Gina's necklace.

I sat back on the toilet lid holding the necklace, feeling Gina's presence. What possible explanation could there be for Mr. Johnson to have Gina's necklace? She was wearing it both times I saw her the week she died. Then I remembered. Tall, handsome, long hair, like a hippie. Gina's strange statements about love making you crazy, and her insistence that she was far from perfect. I took the necklace out and held it in my hands, and I felt pure rage. The instinct that propelled me to his front door suddenly made sense. The dizzying facts and disconnected shards of information came together to form a solid picture. The monster had been right here all along. I heard his voice, and it startled me.

"Everything okay in there, Maggie? I know that bathroom is a mess. Mrs. Johnson stopped using it when she was pregnant because of the kitty litter, and I confess I'm not a very good maid. My apologies," Mr. Johnson called out to me, his voice approximating concern.

"Yeah, I'll be right out," I hollered back.

I frantically cleaned up the mess as best I could and replaced the tin under the sink. I had to get the necklace to the police. But first I had to get out of the house with it. I tried balling it up in my hand, but the letters that spelled Evangelina were wide, and it seemed obvious that I was holding something.

If I had worn a bra, I could've put it in there, but I was still too flat-chested to need a bra, and even though I sometimes wore one just out of pride, today was too hot, and I opted not to. I cursed myself for wearing gym shorts with no pockets. I finally decided I could wedge it between the elastic waistband of my shorts and my chubby belly. At least my chub would finally be useful for something.

I came out of the bathroom slowly, and he was standing right outside the door.

"Sorry about that," I sputtered out an apology, and I could feel my cheeks turning red.

"Are you sure you're okay?" He got closer to me and stared in my face. Then he put his hand on my forehead to see if I was hot, and I had to fight the urge to recoil from his touch.

"I'd just better be going home," I explained with a forced smile.

He eyed me curiously, blocking my way, and I had to maneuver around him. When I did, I could feel the necklace fall down a bit in my shorts; it was now hanging precariously.

"I think I should walk you, Maggie. You look sort of, green." Mr. Johnson laughed a little.

"Nope, I'm good. Just need to get home and take a nap, I think. Like a baby. You know about babies," I was babbling, making little sense. But my heart felt like it was beating out of my chest. I gave Mr. Johnson a silly wave and walked towards the door. I had my hand on the doorknob when I felt the necklace fall onto the floor.

Before I knew it, Mr. Johnson's hands were on my shoulders. I wanted to scream, but I could feel his breath on my neck.

"Maggie, I think you should sit back down on the couch and catch your breath," he said, his voice monotone and menacing.

He guided me toward the couch, and I sat down, still stunned.

I watched him pick up the necklace. Then he closed the storm door. When he turned back around, his face had changed, his eyes darkened. He looked at me suspiciously, trying to ascertain something. I just stared back, but my face must have been revealing. He sighed heavily, looking up at the ceiling.

"Let me get you some water. Perhaps the lemonade was too acidic. You must be dehydrated from the heat and getting sick," he said politely, as if the necklace had never existed. He walked into the kitchen.

I got up and tiptoed to the front door, but he walked back into the room just as I put my hand on the door handle. Our eyes met, and again he guided me back to the couch, more firmly this time.

"I'll walk you home but drink some water first. I don't want you passing out on my sidewalk this time," he smiled as he spoke, as if it was a funny comment.

I took a quick sip of water. My hand was shaking as I lifted the glass to my mouth. Then I stood up.

"I'm good," I announced. He motioned for me to sit back down. I did as he directed, unsure what was happening. I landed on the sofa with a thud, still unsteady on my feet.

"Finish your water and then you can go." He pointed at my water glass. I gulped the glass down, anxious to escape.

Mr. Johnson began to speak in a soft voice, almost to himself.

"I was very fond of Gina," he began. "She was such a lovely girl. She wrote, you know? She was a fine writer. And she was so interested in everything, politics, art, music. I was enjoying teaching her, and she was such an eager student. She especially loved poetry. It takes a special person to love poetry, and Gina was special. My wife is only interested in the baby and television shows," he scoffed condescendingly.

I sat still like a rabbit, with no defense but to freeze.

"I so enjoyed Gina," he added with a sad smile. And I nodded as if I understood what he was talking about.

"But then it got so complicated. Gina wanted more. And she became so irrational, so emotional. Every simple pleasure must have complications," he complained with an exasperated sigh.

He looked at me as if I would understand, so I nodded as if his crazy talk made sense. He was unburdening himself to me. He wanted sympathy from me. It was insane.

"Mr. Johnson, I really should be going home now. My parents will be worried. I'm sorry I came over. It's not my business. I won't say anything about the necklace. I mean, it's just a necklace. Lots of girls have them. I was thinking of getting one," I was rambling on nervously. He ignored me.

I moved toward the edge of the sofa. My mind was racing. If I screamed now, would anyone hear me? I couldn't possibly get to the door without going through him.

"Come on, Maggie. You understand what's happening here. You're a smart girl," Mr. Johnson said dryly.

"Oh, I'm not really that smart. Ask the nuns," I tried to make a joke and laughed a little hysterically.

"Gina and I agreed to keep our relationship a secret. I certainly didn't expect her to tell a child. I misjudged her in so many ways," he said with disdain.

"Gina didn't tell me anything. I don't know anything. I swear," I responded. My voice sounded high and shrill. I didn't even recognize it.

I stood up and started to walk toward the door, but he was quick for a big man, and he guided me back to my seat on the sofa. Then he resumed his soliloquy.

"The pregnancy was the final straw, as they say. I told her she couldn't have a baby. I was supportive, offered to pay for her to get rid of it. I even offered to take her to the appointment," he said with exasperation. He acted as if offering to pay for an abortion was some form of gallantry.

I nodded, afraid that any word I said would provoke an angry reaction. My mind was scrambling, trying to figure a way past him.

"But Gina was so stubborn. She refused to get rid of it, even if I paid. She was being so impossible. She was going to tell Beth, and then the school would know, and I would lose everything," he was still talking in a very calm voice, as if what he was explaining made perfect sense.

"I didn't plan it. It just happened, but afterward I knew it was what had to be done. For my family. It was so difficult," he said sadly, as if he was the one who had suffered. "She left me no choice. It was Gina or I," he stated gravely. And I thought about how strange it was that he would use such precise grammar when describing a murder. But then he was an English teacher. A psychotic, murdering English teacher.

I felt my stomach lurch, and I thought I was going to puke again. "I think I need to use the bathroom again," I mumbled and tried to stand up. But I got woozy and crumbled back on the couch.

"I never fainted before. I don't know what's going on," I felt myself starting to cry. I was in a nightmare, running underwater, getting nowhere.

"Well, the first time was likely the heat. But this time, it's the water you drank," he motioned to the glass on the coffee table. What had he put in the water? The room looked fuzzy.

"Mr. Feeney saw me come in here. He'll tell my parents," I tried a desperate bluff.

"Oh Maggie, do you really think I don't look around when I let pretty girls in my house?" he laughed softly.

I felt my eyes closing. I tried to keep them open, but I couldn't.

Cellars

I was having the dream. I was in the fruit cellar at my grandparents' house. The walls were made of mud, and there were jars of peppers and pickles stacked on wooden shelves. The ladder that led to the outside was missing, and there was rain coming in from the door above.

My grandfather was there, his back to me. I was in my nightgown, and I was terrified. My grandfather turned to face me. He grinned at me under the single lightbulb that hung from the ceiling on a string. His teeth were huge and sharp like a vampire's. I tried to scream, but nothing would come out, and then water started to pour in, and I couldn't breathe.

I startled awake on an old sofa in a cellar. It smelled moldy and damp. I was in darkness with only a scanty streak of sunlight threaded through a small window. I could make out skis, a weathered dresser, and an old pool table with tattered green felt sitting under the window. Pool cues of various sizes stood in a stand next to the table. An old refrigerator hummed near the stairs.

My ankles were tied, and my arms were bound over my head with a rope that was looped around a pipe so I couldn't move. There was duct tape over my mouth. My pants were wet, and I cringed with the realization that I had peed my pants. I would leave this life as humiliated as I had lived it. As my eyes focused, I realized I was not alone. Mr. Johnson was sitting

177

on a straight-back chair, smoking a cigarette and reading a book by flashlight.

"Ah, you're awake," he snapped his book shut. He showed me the cover, *The Beautiful and Damned* by F. Scott Fitzgerald.

"Apropos, don't you think?" he said with a smile.

I stared at him, willing myself to wake up and make this all a dream.

"Daisy is named after a Fitzgerald character," he shared, as if this were a normal conversation two people might have about a book. But, of course, I couldn't contribute to the conversation with duct tape over my mouth.

"I've always had a weakness for beautiful girls, just like good old Scott Fitzgerald. I first read him in high school, and I was infatuated with his prose, the parties, and all the fresh young women," he shared with a sickening smile.

I tried to wriggle myself loose, but it was impossible.

He stretched out his legs and lay back in the chair, staring at the ceiling and blowing smoke upwards.

"You're a complication, Maggie. And as I said before, complications are not good," he sighed. "I'm sorry. But what else can I do?" he asked me, palms upward, as if he was the one in the tough situation.

I stared at him, wondering how someone could sound so calm and rational while being so crazy.

He dropped his cigarette on the concrete floor of the basement and stomped it out with his boot.

"Filthy habit apparently. I have to smoke down here now because my wife doesn't want me smoking around the baby," he sniped with irritation, rolling his eyes.

Then he stood up and came over to me, staring at me with a detached curiosity, like you would a museum exhibit.

"You would have been a pretty girl when you got older. I can see it in your eyes," he gave me a strange and chilling compliment. "You'd lose the baby fat and acquire that alluring confidence girls possess at 16," he smirked.

Then a look of concern crossed his face as if something had suddenly occurred to him.

"You don't look comfortable," he said. He put a pillow under my head, so my arms weren't pulled so taut. It was a strangely tender act for someone who was planning to kill me. I recoiled at his touch, but he didn't seem to notice. He stood back and looked at me again.

"Luckily, my wife is visiting her mother tonight, so you can just rest here until it's time. It's dusk now, so it won't be long." He patted my sneakers and jogged back upstairs, like a man without a care in the world.

My hands were tied too tight for me to move, but my feet were looser. If I could just kick something toward myself to use to cut the ropes, I stood some chance. But I couldn't see anything of use. And the sun was rapidly setting. The light was eerie, casting more shadows than anything. How long had I been passed out?

I lay there and wondered how my family would feel when my body was discovered. Would my mother think it was my fault? Would Mrs. Conway say I was wild and misbehaved? Would the police or newspaper tell people I peed my pants?

I heard noises upstairs. A cat meowed loudly, and I could hear Mr. Johnson talking sweetly to it. I heard dishes clinking as he ate dinner. Then I heard music from his record player. This was madness. How could he pet the cat, eat dinner, and listen to records, passing time until he killed me?

Then the doorbell rang, and voices rumbled. It was a woman's voice with Mr. Johnson. I tried to reach the wall with my feet and kick it to make noise, but my legs were too short. The best I could do was scrape the wall with my sneakers.

Suddenly, I heard a woman's voice, yelling, upset. I realized then it was Cynthia. Was she going to be his next victim? I wanted to warn her, but then I remembered I was his next victim.

Cynthia sounded like she was crying, and then it got quiet. Voices again, and the front door opened. I heard the storm door slam. She was gone. I started to cry. I shut my eyes and prayed to God, to Gina, to anyone who would listen to me.

Eventually, it got very quiet upstairs and dark in the basement. I was completely alone, and I had missed any chance to escape. I would never get to tell the police about the necklace. Mr. Johnson would get away with it. Who knows where he'd toss my body? Maybe no one would ever find it. Maybe my parents would think I ran away. Charlie would rot in jail. I failed Gina. I failed everyone.

All of a sudden, there was movement by the window, and someone pushed it open. A flashlight sprayed light on my face. Then miraculously, I heard someone whisper my name.

"Maggie," a voice hissed. I looked towards the window and saw the shadowed outline of my best friend's face.

I moved around as much as I could so he would see me, and I grunted.

"I see you," he whispered. "I'm coming in."

Soon I saw his skinny body squirm through the window. Richie could wriggle through a keyhole if he set his mind to it. He dangled for a few seconds and then dropped to the pool table under the window. He landed with a thud, and we froze for a moment to see if anyone heard. But it was quiet upstairs.

A flashlight flicked on me, and Richie jumped off the pool table, ran over, and pulled the duct tape off my mouth.

"Ouch," I squealed as the tape burned my face.

"Shush," he said and put his finger to his mouth to remind me.

"It's him! Mr. Johnson killed Gina, and he's going to kill me," I started to spill the facts and I began to cry. But Richie shushed me again.

"I know. I figured it out. I went into Monica's room today to borrow some records, and I found a necklace in between two records, like it fell or was hidden there. It had her name, just like Gina's. I asked her who gave it to her, and she didn't want to tell me, but I made her. And she said Mr. Johnson gave it to her, and she thought it was weird. I thought about what the old man in the jewelry store said about a handsome hippie. Then I called you. Your parents said you weren't home, and they were worried. Then I just knew where you were." He pointed to his head when he said this as if to indicate his amazing powers of deduction.

"How did you find me down here?" I asked, still amazed he was standing in front of me.

"I snuck around the house and looked in the windows. I could see Johnson, but not you. I was starting to think I was wrong or too late or something, and then I saw the basement window. And I finally saw you here," he explained, as he was untying me. The knots were fairly easy for him to unravel, and I hopped to my feet. I felt the relief of movement.

"Wonder Twins," he grinned, and we bumped fists.

"How do we get out of here?" I asked desperately, realizing being untied solved only half the problem. He gestured to the window. I looked at him in disbelief. Why had I eaten so many Moonpies and Twinkies all summer? I would never fit.

"Richie, I can't fit. You go back out. You untied me. I'll fight him off. You get help," I said. He shook his head.

"He's too strong. And what if I can't get anybody in time? No one will believe me," he reasoned and shook his head. We were startled by the sound of the locks on the basement door abruptly opening.

"Lie back down, Maggie. Pretend you're still tied up," Richie whispered, putting the duct tape loosely back over my mouth. Then he ran and hid behind the stairs.

I lay back on the couch and acted as if I couldn't move. I thought Mr. Johnson would hear my heart beating out of my chest. The light flicked on, and a single bulb hanging from the ceiling provided sudden light. Mr. Johnson walked casually down the stairs.

"Time's up, Maggie. There's a nice moon tonight to guide us," he informed me as if this was good news. As he approached me, he noticed my duct tape was slipping off, and a curious smile came over his face.

"Now, how did you manage that?" he asked quizzically.

Richie came flying out from behind the staircase and hit Mr. Johnson in the back of the head with a pool cue. It wasn't enough to knock him out, but enough to stun him. He looked around to see who was there. Richie hit him again, this time in the jaw.

I flew past Mr. Johnson and ran up the stairs, with Richie behind me and Mr. Johnson on our heels. Halfway up the stairs, I heard a grunt. I looked back and saw Mr. Johnson grab Richie, dragging him back down into the basement. Richie was screaming and kicking at him. I saw him bite Mr. Johnson's arm, and Mr. Johnson yelped in pain.

"Run, Maggie!" Richie screamed. But I couldn't leave him after he had rescued me.

I ran back down the stairs and grabbed another pool cue, a shorter one. I swung at Mr. Johnson's face as hard as I could and hit him square on the nose. Blood spurted out, and he instinctively put his hands to his face. He was momentarily dazed. Richie darted up the stairs, and I followed.

As we bounded into the kitchen, Mr. Johnson caught up with me and pulled my hair. I screeched in pain. Richie was kicking him and slugging him with every ounce of power and anger in his little body, but Mr. Johnson was tugging me back in the direction of the basement.

Suddenly, we were all aware of voices in the house, and a police officer's shadow was framed in the archway of the kitchen. For a moment, we all froze. Then suddenly, Mr. Johnson let go of my hair and put his hands up.

Two police officers came bounding into the kitchen and grabbed Mr. Johnson. Next I heard my father's voice. He bolted in, hugged me and Richie, and then rushed us out the front door and down the steps. The rest of our parents were running down the street towards the Johnson house.

Heroes

Richie and I were still panting and dazed on the sidewalk, trying to explain to the police what had happened, how we figured it all out, how Mr. Johnson had put something in my water and tied me up in the basement, and how wiry, little Richie had come to my rescue and hit the monster with a pool cue. Twice! And I had broken his nose with the third thwack.

As we spoke, Richie got more energized, jumping from foot to foot, partly traumatized and partly amazed at his own bravery.

"But how did you guys know to come here?" I asked an officer, still stunned by our good fortune that they had arrived just in time.

It turned out that when Richie took off earlier in the night, Monica got worried. She confessed to Grandma Rose that Mr. Johnson had given her the necklace. He was her English teacher. At first, she really enjoyed his class. Mr. Johnson was so complimentary about her writing, really encouraging her, but soon after he gave her the necklace as a gift. The necklace had upset her, and she had steered clear of him since receiving it. Monica's instincts might have saved her life.

Once Monica told Grandma Rose the whole story — about Mr. Johnson and the necklaces, that Richie and I were investigating Gina's murder, and that Richie had set out to look for me when I wasn't at home — Grandma Rose sprang into action. She called the police, explaining everything, and then my parents, and everyone converged on the Johnsons' house. When there was no answer at the door, the police forced their way inside.

The police put Mr. Johnson in the back of a police car, its red lights flashing, and he looked over at us with a completely blank expression on his face. I remembered that he still had Gina's necklace.

"Did you find Gina's necklace? He had it in the house. With her name? I don't want him to have it anymore. I don't want him to have anything of Gina's anymore. And I have a cigarette butt from the crime scene under my mattress in a baggy. We think it's his," I explained. The cop just looked at me with his mouth open.

Richie and I filled the police in on everything that had happened, from our suspects to the necklaces, to our inspection of the crime scene. As I explained my discovery in Uncle Jimmy's bedroom to the police, my mother's color grew ashen, and she put her hands to her face.

Uncle Jimmy might not be a murderer, but he was definitely some kind of predator. My dad went back to our house to retrieve the cigarette butt and Uncle Jimmy's illicit photos for the police per my instructions, and the cops searched the house for Gina's necklace. It sure felt like Richie, and I were in charge of the investigation.

Finally, after we finished describing our crime-solving expertise and foolhardy bravery, we were allowed to go home.

Richie and I hugged first, and I realized then that he had saved my life. I started to cry.

"You saved me, Richie," I whispered.

"We saved each other. We're the Wonder Twins," he said, grinning at me, and we fist-bumped again. I saw my mother watch us in puzzlement.

The Harpers took Richie home. As their car pulled away, Richie waved at me from the back window, smiling. We had done it.

My parents and I walked home in silence, my dad's arm around my shoulder. I had stopped crying but suddenly felt so tired. Only my sister spoke.

"Holy Crap, Maggie!! I can't believe you did this! You were almost murdered," she hollered, but she was also beaming with a kind of pride at her little sister's courage.

"Please, Patty, don't even say that out loud," my mother said softly, and I noticed silent tears on her face.

We went inside, and my mother immediately got me a ginger ale. My father called my pediatrician to ask about whatever Mr. Johnson had put in my water, but the doctor said as long as I was okay now, I could wait until tomorrow to get checked out.

We sat around the kitchen table, and I explained everything that had happened. My mother was silent at the revelations about her brother, and I had no idea if she would ever forgive me. When I got to the part about the basement, I started to cry, realizing how horrible it had been, how terrified I was.

When I was done talking, I suddenly felt exhausted. Patty and I hugged our parents good night and walked upstairs together.

"Wanna sleep in my Kinks t-shirt, Mags?" Patty offered kindly. "It always gives me great dreams," she added with a smile. Since the Kinks t-shirt was practically sacred to Patty, I knew she must have really been scared for me.

"Sure," I said, and she fetched it from her room. I put it on and climbed into bed. Patty looked at herself in the mirror on the back of my door for a minute.

"Do you think you will be able to sleep, Mags?" she asked, her voice full of concern.

"I think so. Night, Patty," I said with a yawn.

"Night, Mags. Sweet dreams only. You are wearing the blessed shirt," she announced and made the Sign of the Cross in the air. Then she winked at me and left. I pulled my covers up tight.

I was more exhausted than I had ever been in my life. I held Sonny and Cher tight, no longer ashamed of having dolls, or frizzy hair, or any other part of being me. I said my prayers, and then I talked to Gina.

"I'm so sorry Gina about what happened to you. I hope you can have peace now that he can't hurt anyone else, and Charlie will be home. I love you very much, and I always will," I whispered.

Then I fell into a deep sleep, and the only dream I had was a beautiful one. We were all on our street together, laughing, like old times...Gina, Charlie, Patty, Monica, Richie, and me. The sun was shining, and we were happy the way we had been before all the monsters.

Afterward

One week later, Thursday, July 13, 1972

Mr. Johnson was denied bail and would sit in jail until his trial. The police talked to the school he had worked at in Indiana and found out that he had been fired from that job for a relationship with a high school girl. Three other girls in town came forward to say he had given them necklaces, attempting to lure them into relationships.

The evidence in the murder was equally damning. In addition to Gina's necklace, the police found the jacket Gina had been wearing at the diner that night in the trunk of Mr. Johnson's car. He had killed her in his car, strangled her, and dumped her body on Pirate's Island in the dark. Mr. Johnson, with his feathered hair and Colgate smile, was a demon, living right on my street.

Mrs. Johnson packed up her baby in her yellow VW Bug and drove back to her parents' house, and no one ever heard from her again.

Eventually a "For Sale" sign appeared outside the house. But I couldn't imagine anyone would want to live there, in that house where a murderer had lived. The house still spooked me, especially the basement window, and I always blessed myself when I walked by.

Uncle Jimmy was fired from his position at the high school, but no formal charges were brought against him. When I told Richie, he said Grandma Rose called it "white man's justice." She was right. If Uncle

Jimmy had been Black, I'm sure it would've been different. He got a new job as the night janitor at a nearby men's prison, where there was little opportunity to take pictures of anything but convicts, who probably wouldn't appreciate Uncle Jimmy's photography hobby.

We stopped going to Grandma's house on Sunday after church. After a few weeks passed, she came to our house instead, without Uncle Jimmy. I don't know if shame kept Uncle Jimmy from our house or if my father had banished him. Either way was fine with me. Grandma and I never discussed what I had found, but from then on, I always heard a tinge of anger in her voice when she spoke to me.

My mother and I never revisited the unpleasant discovery about her beloved brother; she still spoke of him with fondness as if it had never happened. And I never told my mother anything more about my grandfather, but I also didn't need her to believe me anymore. I knew what was true, and that was enough.

For the first time, I started wondering about my mother's childhood. Maybe she wanted our family to appear perfect so no one would ever see the terrible secrets she was keeping. I guess it's hard to give up a lie when it's so much better than the truth. And maybe when you're pretending and hiding, it's safer to keep people at a distance. I started to think that the reason my mother couldn't love me was because no one had ever taught her how.

But something in my relationship with my mother had changed. She wasn't any warmer; that would never be her personality. And we would never agree on social skills or my friends. But after everything that happened, she left me more or less alone, and stopped trying to control my life.

Whether she realized I was growing up, or she had just given up all hope for me, I wasn't sure. But I had defied her, and I had been proven right. She would never admit it, but inside, she knew. And somehow that had fundamentally shifted the balance in our relationship. I was no longer a project to be worked on, but a force to be reckoned with. And for my mother, respect was the nearest thing to love you could ask for.

Patty's mission to attend public school was over with a definitive "no" from our mother, who said Patty needed to "cool her heels." After the revelation about Mr. Johnson, a public-school teacher, Patty seemed a bit less certain she wanted to go there anyway.

Patty was shocked into a temporary lull by the news about Mr. Johnson. She did remark with her usual flippancy, "I used to have such a crush on Mr. Johnson. It's insane. Well, I guess I'm glad the loser never gave me a necklace. But to think he gave Cynthia one! That's proof positive he's a psychopath. Her ass is the size of Texas."

After the events of this summer, Patty and I would both be lucky if we didn't end up in a convent for cloistered nuns in September.

Ironically, a few days after our mother's edict about Catholic school, Father Anthony was transferred to another parish after a parent two streets over, not a Catholic, complained about his driving around at night talking to kids. My parents were angered by his relocation, but I wondered if another monster had just been ejected from our orbit.

One day as I was aimlessly riding my bike around the neighborhood, I saw Ray's car parked in front of the Johnsons' house. I walked over to him and underneath his sunglasses, I could tell he was crying. I was dumbstruck; I just stood there staring at him.

"I never liked that asshole," he motioned toward the house. "I told Gina, but she wouldn't listen. He snowed her, and she wasn't the only girl."

I thought about Ray watching Cynthia, and it made sense now. He was worried about her. I had him all wrong.

"I know," I said, nodding my head, but he was lost in his own story. He needed to tell someone. It seemed strange that he chose me, but then I thought about how I had never seen him with anyone but Gina. He must have been so lonely without her.

"We fought about her babysitting for him. But I saw the way he looked at her, and it skeeved me out. He's the reason she dumped me. I knew something was up with them, but she denied it. I should've stopped her." He took off his sunglasses and wiped his nose with a red bandanna.

"No one could stop Gina when she was determined to do something," I tried to comfort him.

"Yeah, she was super stubborn. She was always changing the radio station in my car to hear the Carpenters. I always hated the Carpenters. Now when one of their songs comes on, I listen. I feel like it's Gina talking to me," he confessed.

I just smiled.

"I guess that's stupid," he added with an embarrassed laugh.

"Nah, that totally sounds like something Gina would do to drive you crazy," I reassured him with a smile.

"She really loved you, ya know," he added, and I could see how sad his eyes were.

"She was the best," I said.

"She really was. I really loved her. Take care of yourself, Maggie," he said softly, and then he drove slowly away. I felt guilty about Ray. He wasn't a monster at all, just someone who probably learned early that it was safer to look tough in a dangerous world. Later that day, I heard "Close to You" by the Carpenters, and I thought of Gina and smiled.

Charlie never got a formal apology from the police, but a newspaper article revealed the police had no evidence against him at all, except that he was the last person Gina was seen with, and he was Black. That Friday night, Gina had been upset and Charlie had tried, good friend that he was, to talk to her. But she was keeping a secret that she couldn't tell him.

Charlie knew she was pregnant but had no idea the baby's father was Mr. Johnson; he assumed it was Ray. When Charlie told Gina she had to confront Ray and demand support, she became angry with him. That's why they were fighting in the diner.

After driving around for a while, he dropped her off on her front porch, and never saw her again. Richie said Charlie blamed himself that Gina hadn't trusted him with the truth. I hoped he would let that go. The only person who was to blame was Mr. Johnson. He must have picked her up after Charlie left. But, of course, no one saw that or ever would've suspected a handsome, white English teacher.

No one in town apologized for assuming Charlie was guilty. All my mother said was, "Well, who would've expected it was that teacher with such a lovely wife." The town believed the Harpers would have to understand that it was an honest mistake. In the minds of the town, it wasn't their fault the police arrested the wrong man. Never mind that Charlie was so sweet, a great student, a hard worker, and that the whole town had known him since he was born. They readily chose to believe he was a murderer.

The first time I rode my bike over to Richie's house after Mr. Johnson was arrested, Charlie answered the door, but didn't open the screen or invite me inside.

But there was more than just a screen between us. I was on the other side of some invisible, but very solid, wall. I was now acutely aware that I was not a part of their family. I was part of the world that hurt them.

I noticed Charlie had purple bruises around his eye and on his cheek bone. I tried not to stare. I wondered how he got those bruises, and guilt flooded me. Charlie smiled at me, but it was a low watt smile that didn't reach his eyes. I wondered if he would ever smile that blindingly bright smile again.

"Hey, Maggie May," he said.

"Hi, Charlie. I missed you," I said shyly.

"Thanks for what you did," he said softly, so subdued. When he looked at me, I could see pain in his eyes where before there had always been joy.

"Richie did all the hard stuff," I reminded him.

As if by magic, Richie appeared behind Charlie when I spoke his name.

Charlie opened the door to let Richie out, giving me a quick hug before retreating back into the house. The hug gave me hope that maybe I would someday be back in the Harpers' house as I had been before.

Richie and I sat on the lawn and stared at each other, still in disbelief, unsure what to do now. In the span of a few days, we had aged so much. But eventually, our energy won out over any newfound maturity, and we got on our bikes and rode through the streets of our town, as we had done before everything went wrong. I felt free and happy with Richie by my side.

When I arrived home that day, I found my father sitting on the front steps of our house. I was worried there had been a fight, but he smiled and waved at me.

"Hey Kiddo, how are you holding up?" he asked, standing up to hug me. Then he sat back down, patting the step to invite me to join him. It was odd behavior for my dad, but then everything in the past week had been odd, so I just sat.

"I'm okay. Actually, I feel pretty good," I replied, smiling at the thought of Charlie now free and clear. We sat in companionable silence, watching the street for a few minutes.

Then my father cleared his voice and spoke, "I'm sorry, Maggie. I was wrong to jump to that conclusion about Charlie." I tried to hide my surprise. I had never heard either of my parents admit to being wrong about anything before.

"Did you really think he would hurt Gina?" I asked, still incredulous that anyone could have thought that.

He sighed deeply and sat in thought for a moment.

"I didn't know. I only knew that I saw them together, and at the time, it seemed incriminating. But I should've thought about Charlie and what a good kid he's always been," he admitted and shook his head.

"Incriminating means made him look guilty," he explained as an afterthought.

"I know what it means," I replied.

My dad chuckled softly. "Ah, yes, I forgot, you are a detective now," he answered with a smile. He sat for a minute and then took a deep breath.

"If you would go with me, I'd like to apologize to the Harpers in person," he asked. I was both touched and surprised by his desire to make amends.

"I would definitely do that," I promised.

"Good. Because they deserve that at the very least," he said softly.

"They do," I agreed.

"Maggie, what you said about your grandfather...you can talk to me about anything," his voice broke a bit, and he trailed off. I felt myself freeze in disbelief. For so long I had wanted to talk to someone about that, but I couldn't do it. At least not yet. My eyes filled with tears.

"Okay," I whispered, and he nodded in understanding.

"Whenever you're ready, I'm here," he said. I knew this was as hard for him as it was for me. We were not a family that talked about real things. It would take some getting used to.

My dad gave me another quick hug. Then, he stood up abruptly and surveyed the front yard.

"Looks like I need to mow," he announced and walked down the steps to the garage to retrieve the lawnmower.

As the sun slowly set, I watched my dad criss-cross our small front lawn, making neat rows out of unruly grass, and I felt grateful for all the people I loved so much.

Eclipse

August, 1972

The rest of the summer passed uneventfully. The Presidential Conventions, the Watergate Scandal, even the Vietnam War were just things our parents talked about; they didn't faze us after what we had seen in our own town.

For a short time after Richie and I solved the mystery of Gina's death, we were heroes with our fickle peers, but within weeks, our halos faded, and we were once again outcasts. But I didn't care because I knew the truth: They were the monsters, not us.

My father and I did go to the Harpers to apologize. My mother even made two pies for us to take, but she said she was too tired to go with us. Still, it was something. Although the conversation was awkward at first, after some coffee and pie, we were all laughing, and Charlie and my dad even hugged before we left.

My parents started taking walks in the evening together and seemed to be drinking a bit less. Whether the peace would last, I didn't know. It would never be a perfect marriage, but it was theirs to figure out.

Now it was August and fall loomed.

The final big event of the summer was the eclipse. Though it seemed like a bit of an afterthought now, Richie and I were still curious to see the moon hide the sun at midday. Just as my dad had said, the government advised people not to stare directly at the sky during the eclipse. We were to cover our heads with boxes and only look around us, not up. Apparently, during the 1960 eclipse, some people went blind staring at the sky.

Just before two pm, Richie appeared on my front steps, a Bush's Baked Beans box atop his head with two holes cut out for his eyes. I laughed when I saw him, then realized I looked just as silly in my Del Monte Canned Corn box. We were an advertisement for a cookout. By 2:05, the whole neighborhood was out on the street wandering around with boxes on heads.

The eclipse snuck up quickly, until before I knew it, it was relatively dark outside. I looked through the holes in my box and saw my neighbors, my mother, my sister, and Richie.

Hiding. We were all hiding under our boxes, shadows in the sudden darkness of the moon.

I thought about how little I really knew about what was inside anyone. And how easy it seemed to be for the darkness to eclipse the light. The masks that came over people when you least expected it and then disappeared just as fast, leaving you bewildered at who anyone really was.

The eclipse was over in minutes, and we all took off our boxes, a bit dazed, and scurried back to our houses. Richie and I sat on my front steps in companionable silence, awed at the universe and how much we didn't know about life, the Milky Way, and the people around us.

Eventually, wonder gave way to hunger, and we rode our bikes to Richie's house. Grandma Rose had promised us ice cream cones after the eclipse.

So, summer ended as it had begun. Richie and I sitting on his front steps, eating chocolate ice cream, piled high on sugar cones, courtesy of Grandma Rose. The sun was warm, but the chill in the air was hinting at autumn. The street was quiet and peaceful, and it seemed hard to believe the events of the summer had ever happened.

"Richie, do you really think we will live in New York in a fancy apartment?" I asked him. I was in a contemplative mood with junior high starting in three days.

"Absolutely," he said, with a renewed confidence.

"And we will always be friends?" I asked him.

"Are you crazy? Of course! Best friends!" he yelled. Then he stood up suddenly, struck by a thought.

"What's the matter?" I asked, jolted by his sudden jump to his feet.

"I forgot something in the house," he hollered, as he ran back inside, the screen door slapping loudly behind him.

I sat on the steps alone for a moment and enjoyed the peace I always found at Richie's house.

A few minutes later, Richie came bounding out the front door with a present wrapped messily in pink tissue paper.

"For you." He bowed with goofy formality and handed me the present.

"But it's not my birthday or anything," I protested, feeling suddenly embarrassed by the kindness.

"It's a thank-you gift from me and Charlie, for everything you did," Richie said gently, tears welling up in his eyes, my big-hearted friend.

"Open it, Maggie!" He nudged my shoulder and plopped down next to me.

I tore the tissue paper apart to find a beautiful journal with a picture of the New York City skyline at night on the cover.

"I love it, Richie!" I cried, delighted.

"It's for your stories," he explained. As I felt my own eyes beginning to tear up, Richie hugged me tight.

"Thank you, Richie. It's perfect," I told him.

"Hey, no crying. Jeez." He poked me, as if I was the only soppy one. Then he got up and started dancing on the sidewalk in front of me, listening to music in his head as he always did.

At that moment, I realized I had always been afraid, my whole life. But I wasn't anymore.

It was true there were monsters in the world, and they rarely looked like you imagined. They lived among us, hiding in plain sight, smiling and pretending that they didn't have fangs, or claws, or hearts of stone.

But now I knew the monsters could be defeated. Bad things did happen, but good things happened, too. And I was right all along about what mattered and what was true. All you really need in life is one true friend. Whatever came next, I would be fine because I had Richie.

Richie pulled me up to dance with him. My moves hadn't improved any, but I didn't care. I jumped around, and when I shut my eyes, I swore I could hear the music too.

Acknowledgements

I would first like to thank my husband Harlan, my best friend and biggest fan. Thank you for encouraging my writing and loving my characters. Thank you to my sweet daughters Elizabeth and Caroline. Being your mom is the greatest privilege and joy of my life. I am always inspired by you to do better.

I am grateful to my lifelong friend, my sister, Mary Ellen Mamone, for reading the manuscript, giving advice, and allowing me to share parts of our childhood in the story.

I am lucky to have amazing English teacher colleagues who were willing to read and critique my manuscript and offer many helpful suggestions: Catherine Curvin, Samantha DiPace, Joseph Kott, Sarah Quinn, Jami Sautter, and Jordan White.

Thanks to my students who knew I was attempting to write a book and were so encouraging and excited for me, and who remind me every day of the excitement and turmoil of growing up.

Great thanks to Abby Macenka at Between the Lines for taking a chance on a first-time novelist and making this dream come true, and Amber Soha for her expertise in editing my manuscript. A thank you to Penny Dowden for her skilled proofreading. Deepest thanks to Cherie Fox for the breathtaking cover art. You captured Maggie and Richie so perfectly.

Finally, I would like to add a thank you to any reader who finds this book. Knowing you might read the words I wrote fills me with a gratitude that is hard to describe. I hope this book reminds you that no matter what your past, the future is always wide open. A difficult childhood does not have to define your life. Wonderful things can still happen. I am proof of that. You just need some good people in your corner and faith in the future. So, forge ahead with confidence and never forget how much you matter.

Eileen Riley Hall is a veteran middle and high school English teacher with 25+ years' experience teaching an amazing cast of real-life characters. She previously published a book with Jessica Kingsley Publishers, entitled *Parenting Girls on the Autism Spectrum: Overcoming the Challenges and Celebrating the Gifts*. The book is based in part on her experience raising two spectacular daughters on the spectrum. She frequently writes Op-Eds about education, autism, and empathy. She has been published in the *New York Times*, the *New York Post*, and her hometown newspaper *The Times Union*, in addition to multiple autism publications. In life and in literature, she loves championing the underdogs and seeing them triumph against the odds.

Printed in the USA
CPSIA information can be obtained
at www.ICGtesting.com
LVHW041120090224
771078LV00013B/1486